SPECIAL MESSAGE TO READERS

THE ULVERSCROFT FOUNDATION
(registered UK charity number 264873)

was established in 1972 to provide funds for research, diagnosis and treatment of eye diseases. ‹amples of major projects funded by the Ulverscroft Foundation are:-

e Children's Eye Unit at Moorfields Eye ›spital, London

e Ulverscroft Children's Eye Unit at Great mond Street Hospital for Sick Children

ınding research into eye diseases and ·atment at the Department of Ophthalmology, niversity of Leicester

ıe Ulverscroft Vision Research Group, stitute of Child Health

vin operating theatres at the Western phthalmic Hospital, London

ıe Chair of Ophthalmology at the Royal ıstralian College of Ophthalmologists

ın help further the work of the Foundation making a donation or leaving a legacy. ' contribution is gratefully received. If you d like to help support the Foundation or ıire further information, please contact:

: ULVERSCROFT FOUNDATION
e Green, Bradgate Road, Anstey
Leicester LE7 7FU, England
Tel: (0116) 236 4325

v. ›site: www.foundation.ulverscroft.com

Paul Bennett was born in London and educated at Alleyn's School in Dulwich. He studied economics at Exeter University and spent seven years in advertising before setting up a market research agency, which he sold in 1986. He is now semi-retired in order to pursue writing. Bennett lives in a converted barn in Essex with his wife and two daughters.

KILLER IN BLACK

In a small town in Texas, five ex-mercenaries reunite when one of their number, Red — half-Comanche, half-Texan — is threatened. The town's sheriff won't risk his job by helping, so it's down to Johnny Silver and his band of comrades to sort the matter out. The resultant attacks escalate from a simple poisoning of a ranch's water supply, to full-scale war with a fifty-strong gang of bikers. And pulling the strings is their most formidable foe yet — a professional assassin, the Killer in Black. Is Johnny's team still strong enough to take on the challenges posed by their enemy? Or have they finally met their match?

Books by Paul Bennett
Published by The House of Ulverscroft:

MERCENARY

PAUL BENNETT

KILLER IN BLACK

Complete and Unabridged

ULVERSCROFT
Leicester

First published in Great Britain in 2013 by
Robert Hale Limited
London

First Large Print Edition
published 2014
by arrangement with
Robert Hale Limited
London

A catalogue record for this book is available from the British Library.

ISBN 978–1–4448–1962–5

Published by
F. A. Thorpe (Publishing)
Anstey, Leicestershire

Set by Words & Graphics Ltd.
Anstey, Leicestershire
Printed and bound in Great Britain by
T. J. International Ltd., Padstow, Cornwall

This book is printed on acid-free paper

But down these mean streets a man
must go who is not himself mean,
who is neither tarnished nor afraid.

Raymond Chandler

Prologue

The town of Gdentsa, Serbian-Bosnian border — 1995

Our orders were to hold the bridge until it could be blown, thereby cutting off the advance guard of the enemy troops. Shouldn't be difficult. Horatius had defended the bridge at Rome against a whole army. And we were five. Mercenaries all. Bull, the Jamaican; Pieter, the South African; Red, the half-Comanche Texan, and Stanislav, the Pole. And in charge of this merry band? Me, Johnny Silver. Not so much the black sheep of the mighty Silver merchant-banking family, but the lone white sheep among a flock of black.

Our advantage over the enemy was that the five of us were all highly trained — Israeli army for me, Bull in Britain, and their respective national forces for the others. The Serbians, who were advancing rapidly, were mostly irregulars, as were the oppressed Muslims we were being paid by.

The bridge was around 200 feet long with two pairs of pillars each side of a central arch. Below, a river flowed swiftly after the first rains of the autumn. We were stretched out flat at the hump of the bridge so that we could see the enemy and couldn't be seen by them. Behind us a small party of the local militia were attaching explosive charges to each of the pillars. The air was cool and in it hung that eerie quiet that always seems to fall before battle commences. We checked our assault rifles for the third time — anything to make the waiting easier.

We were armed with the old-fashioned Russian Kalashnikov AK-47s, heavy to carry about and notorious for jamming at awkward moments — which was all the time when you're in a fight. I would have preferred my favourite Uzi — shorter, lighter and with a bigger 40-bullet magazine — but they were scarce in these parts. The Kalashnikovs had a theoretical range of 300 metres, but you had to be aiming at a barn before you could be confident of a direct hit at that distance.

And how did we get in this position? The call had come out from the Bosnian Muslims that they needed all the help they could get to prevent genocide by the Serbs, and we had nothing better to do. Plus we were broke. But it seemed a good cause and that always makes fighting easier.

Red, with his inherited Comanche eyesight, was the first of us to notice the advance. The enemy was approaching in a line of five files, just narrow enough to fit on the bridge without breaking step and reforming. I gave the order and we opened fire, aiming at legs rather than bodies since we didn't have to kill, just had to stop their progress. The first file went down. An order was shouted and the second file stepped over the first and marched on. The third file followed and then the next. Seemed like the enemy thought its troops were expendable in the larger scheme of things. Time to get moving.

I looked back and saw the final preparations being made to blow the explosive charges.

'Couple more volleys,' I shouted. 'Then we get out as quickly as possible.'

We opened fire, still aiming low and produced a slow-down of the column. But they still came on.

'OK, let's go,' I shouted.

But the words were lost in the thundering explosion. The ill-disciplined troops had panicked and blown the bridge. Behind us the two pairs of pillars collapsed, taking the road over the bridge with them. Our exit was cut off. There was only one route out.

'Time to swim for it, lads,' I called above the noise of the collapsing brickwork.

Red looked at me anxiously. 'I can't swim,' he said.

‘This is a hell of a time to tell me,’ I said. ‘I thought everyone could swim nowadays.’

‘What reason would a Comanche brave have to swim? We live on the plains.’

‘Hell,’ I said. ‘Well, can’t be a better time to learn. Dump the rifles and let’s go. Bull, you go first and wait for Red. Stan, Pieter, you next. I’ll follow Red down.’

‘But . . . ’ Red started to say, his courage about to fail him.

I grabbed him by the collar of his uniform and swung him round and down through the gap caused by the first pillar collapsing. I jumped an instant after.

I went under and propelled myself up. The water was cold and we wouldn’t be able to survive for long: hypothermia would set in within fifteen minutes or so. There was a strong current trying to carry us downstream. And where was Red?

‘Johnny,’ Bull called.

Bull had his arm around Red’s chin and was trying to keep him afloat. Red was struggling. He’d take Bull down with him if he didn’t stop.

I swam across, the weight of the sodden uniform slowing me down. Red was thrashing about, fighting Bull’s effort to keep him up.

‘Sorry,’ I apologized in advance to Red. ‘But one day you’ll thank me for this.’

There was little I could do but choose my spot. I threw a right hook and hit him hard above the left ear. If he'd been standing upright he would have staggered. In the water his head just lolled back and he went limp. Mission accomplished.

I put a hand under his right armpit and Bull did the same to his left. We moved slowly through the water, heading for the south bank of the river. Then the bullets started raining down. This wasn't going to work. They would gun us down before we could reach the shore. Bull looked at me, reading my mind. We turned Red around and let the current take us, speeding our progress with the best strokes we could manage under the circumstances. Somehow we made it out of range, and a bend in the river put us as close to the shore as we were ever going to get. Then we struck out again. Exhausted, we dragged ourselves up a muddy bank and lay there panting.

We had made it.

And the moral of the story? Despite appearances, know who your friends are and who are your enemies.

1

The island of St Jude, Caribbean.
The present day

'We need to talk, Johnny,' Anna said, the furrow of a frown marring the fine bone-structure of her face. 'We need to talk now.'

This had all the signs of bad news. Her hands were on her hips for a start.

'Is it about Red?' I asked. 'Don't you want me to go?'

'He came to your aid when you called. You cannot let him down.' Anna was from Chechnya and despite having good English she wasn't into idioms and came across as a tad formal at times. 'To not answer his call would be without honour and I know that honour means a great deal to you.'

'It's the mercenary code. Support your buddies, even unto death. I couldn't desert him and live with myself. Couldn't look at my face in the mirror.' I paused and returned her frown. 'If it's not about Red, then what is it, Anna?'

I racked my brains for a reason she might be worried or unhappy. As far as I was concerned life couldn't have been better. Here I was, living the easy life, running a bar on the beach of an idyllic island where the sun shone the whole year round and the sea was a vivid blue. And I had Anna by my side. She was three months pregnant with our first child and blooming. Her hazel eyes sparkled. Her long dark hair had been bleached by the sun to blonde streaks and she looked a million dollars with long, tanned legs in cut-off shorts and stomach still taut in a crop top.

'It's the gun,' she said.

'Ah,' I said, puzzled. 'Anything particular about it?'

'The fact that you've still got it. Every time I go behind the bar I can see it there, taped on the underside. You don't need it any more. Get rid of it, please, Johnny.'

'There's no harm in it. It helps me feel safe and that I can protect you if needs be.'

'Who would want to do us harm? The Russians are not hunting you any more — they're not even alive any more — you saw to that. Since the shoot out in Amsterdam, the only threat to us has been removed.'

She was right. I knew that. We were safe here. The Russians had been defeated in a gunfight orchestrated by me between them and their American mafia counterparts. There was no one looking for us now. St Jude wasn't a hideaway any longer, it was a home. It was just that I would feel naked without the gun. Stupid, I know. But through all my days as a mercenary, and before that in the Israeli army, I had always had some sort of weapon — usually more than one: my favourite Uzi and a Browning Hi-Power handgun.

'What if I keep it in the house?'

'Johnny!'

'OK. OK. I'll get rid of it.' If ever the need arose, there was always Bull's shotgun.

Bull kept a boat on the dock opposite the bar and ran fishing trips for the tourists. He had a shotgun hidden away in the engine compartment. Old habits die hard.

I took two cold beers from the fridge and wandered across to the boat where he was swabbing the decks in advance of a party arriving from the hotel. Normally, the first reaction of his trippers was a stunned silence. Bull was six foot six with a shaved head and muscles that rippled on his ebony body.

And he walked with a limp where the Russians had hamstrung him in Angola.

My memento of the botched mission to Angola was a star-shaped collection of scars where six bullets had ripped out the muscles in my left shoulder. We made a fine pair. Each morning we would swim half a mile up the shore and jog back to the bar for a cold beer — he outpaced me on the swim, where my arm power let me down, then I caught up on the jog, where it was his turn to struggle.

'Take a break,' I said, handing him a beer.

He held the bottle against his forehead and then took a swig.

'I wondered how long it would be,' he said.

'How long what would be?'

'Before Anna got to you.'

'Ah,' I said.

'Yep,' he said. 'Ah.'

'Mai Ling had a word with you,' I guessed.

He nodded. 'United front and pick us off one by one.'

'Good strategy,' I said.

'Too good for us,' he said, breaking into a deep laugh that resonated off the polished wood of the deck.

'Deadlier than the male,' I said.

'Good job we never met any female mercenaries,' he said. 'We'd be stretched out in our graves by now, staring up at tombstones.'

'Reckon so,' I said.

'Maybe they're jittery, too,' he added.

'Wouldn't blame them. We don't know yet what we're getting into. Red was pretty vague on the phone, like he thought the line might be tapped. But then again he always did have a vivid imagination.'

'Whatever it is,' Bull said, shaking his head, 'let's just pray he's not going to drive us anywhere.'

Red's style of driving was to have either the brake or the accelerator pressed right down to the floor. He thought he was the best driver in the world. We knew he was the worst. Still, so far he hadn't managed to kill us.

A thought struck me.

'What did you do with the shotgun?'

Bull smiled. 'I buried it in the garden in a waterproof bag.'

I smiled back. 'Maybe they're not so smart after all.'

* * *

'What did you do with the gun?' Anna said. 'Didn't bury it, like Bull?'

'Would I do that?'

'Just the sort of sneaky thing you would do.'

I sighed. 'All right, I'll dig it up and throw it in the sea. When I get back. If you should need it while I'm away, it's to the right of the fridge in the bar.'

I was packing clothes in a bergan, a kind of supersized rucksack with a multitude of outside pockets capable of taking several magazines of bullets. Anna was folding the clothes in neat bundles and passing them to me. I stuffed them in, filling all the gaps.

'This is going to be the first time we have been apart since we moved here,' I said. 'Four months of living and working together, although you can hardly call the beach bar work. I shall miss you.

She moved closer and put her arms around me. She kissed me long and lingering.

'Let's leave the rest of the packing till the morning,' she said.

* * *

I woke early and lay on the bed with Anna cradled in my arms, her head on my chest. I stared through the window of the long narrow cabin that was our home until we managed to build something bigger and better, and watched the bloom of red expand in the sky as the sun rose. I never tired of this spectacle. I wondered what the rising sun looked like in Texas — could anything be as beautiful as this? Maybe we all thought that our own sunrise was the best in world. Home is where the heart is.

I eased myself from underneath Anna, put on some shorts and a T-shirt and went out to sit on the jetty, where Bull was making his boat safe while we were away.

'Any second thoughts?' he said.

'About Red, no. About me, yes.'

'Don't go all cryptic on me. You know I'm just a simple soul.'

'Wherever we were fighting in the past I only had myself to think about. Now I have Anna. I don't know what effect that will have on my actions. I'd hate to think I might put any of you at risk because I felt the need to pull away from danger — playing it safe because of my other responsibilities.'

'Comforting thought,' he said.

'Sorry,' I replied. Maybe it would have been better to keep my doubts to myself rather than risk them becoming contagious. 'Hell,' I said. 'We function on instinct a lot of the time, that instinct won't change. It's never simply just been about self-preservation. Loyalty to each other — to the group of us — has been a big factor. That won't change.'

'Good to hear it,' he said. 'I'll think of that when you're guarding my back. We've got a long journey in front of us. I hope you're not going to be philosophical all the way.'

'Just had to get it out of my system.'

'I know,' he said. 'I've been here before, remember?'

Bull had a beautiful wife, Mai Ling, and a son aged three years, Michael, whose heart transplant had been funded by our last operation in Amsterdam. They hadn't affected his actions in the heat of battle, so why should Anna affect mine?

'Come on,' I said. 'One last swim before we hit the plains that Red is always going on about.'

'No swimming there,' he said.

'But what will we find to do instead?'

'Cause a whole lot of trouble for someone, I expect.'

2

Our journey started with catching the hotel's shuttle launch to Barbados. We stuck out like sore thumbs among the guests finishing their holidays, clad in their brightly coloured clothes, laughing and chattering, high on the endorphin surge produced by a great holiday. It wasn't just our clothes and solemn demeanour that made us stand out. My father, Gus, had said that there was something about our eyes, Bull and me. Something cold and calculating. Something that said not to mess with us because the consequences could be fatal. It was as if we had become different people from the moment we had left the island. We were no longer the laid-back guys who ran a beach bar and fishing trips; our systems were now moving to the alert like boxers with their weight on their toes ready to strike. And our bergans were out of place among the designer luggage. Our clothes — chinos, boots and T-shirts with cutaway sleeves — were functional rather than frivolous.

The second leg was a flight to Dallas Fort Worth where the other business class travellers avoided our gaze — after the Russian episode we had more than enough money to afford the luxuries of life. Even the flight attendant wouldn't look us in the eye.

From there it was a connecting flight to El Paso, where we stood a chance of losing ourselves among the cowboy mentality of past times; just two guns for hire.

We collected our bags from the carousel and made our way to the main concourse. As in all airports, there were many more people than it had been designed for. We progressed as fast as we could among the throng. The exit was in view when a tall ginger-haired man of about fifty pushed his way past Bull.

'Out of the way, boy,' he said.

Anyone who addresses Bull as 'boy' had better watch out.

Bull dumped his bergan on the ground and started to move after the man. I caught his arm and pulled him back.

'Easy, Bull. Easy,' I said. 'Let's at least try to get out of the airport before we have a fight. If we meet him again, then you can treat him to a lesson in manners.'

There was a young woman and two girls standing just outside the exit doors. The woman was in her late teens or early twenties, long blonde hair, natural tan, wearing a maxi-length flowing dress in a large flower print: it was like watching a documentary about the swinging sixties. The two girls, only just teenagers it looked like, wore jeans, T-shirts and trainers. One was dark-skinned, the other had the milky white skin of an English rose. They were handing out leaflets.

Until the ginger-haired man strode past, that was.

He brushed the woman aside, knocking her and her leaflets to the floor, then he was gone.

Bull and I reached her and helped her get back on to her feet. The two girls picked up the leaflets.

'Are you all right?' I asked.

She brushed a little dirt from her long dress and rose to her full height. She was tall and slim and her natural beauty — bone structure, turned-up nose, high cheekbones — seemed to radiate out. You felt like standing back to take in the full view and then going 'Wow!'.

'Thank you,' she said. 'The senator doesn't let anybody get in his way.'

'The senator?'

'Yes. Senator O'Hara. Hard not to recognize him with that mop of ginger hair. He's one of our neighbours, too, though we don't see much of him. He doesn't agree with what we're doing.'

'And that is?'

'Cameron,' she said to the dark-skinned girl, 'Lucy,' to the other girl, 'give the gentlemen a leaflet each.'

It was an amateur effort, text running over pictures in places, images askew, a few spelling mistakes; it had a homegrown quality about it, but a sense of pride seemed to go with it. The basic message was that you should go to the Alamo Retreat to rediscover yourself; to shed the burden of modern-day life and live as part of a self-supporting community. It didn't mention anything about money — how much you would have to pay for such a rebirth, but my instinct told me that it wasn't going to come cheap. Perhaps my cynicism would be proved wrong, but I doubted it. That's the way of the world.

'I'm Fey,' the woman said, shaking our hands. 'Are you here for business or pleasure?'

I looked at Bull and he grinned. 'Pleasure,' I said. 'Always pleasure.'

'Be sure to come and visit us. Maybe we can help you.'

'I reckon we're both beyond redemption,' I said.

Outside the airport I saw Red leaning back on the door of a big utility vehicle. It looked solid and that, given Red's driving, was reassuring. Red was a little under six foot with jet-black hair, a dark complexion, which came from his half Comanche roots, and big brown eyes. He was dressed like an extra in a John Wayne movie; denim jeans and cowboy boots, plaid shirt and a big hat. Even his glasses — round, wire-framed — looked authentic. He took a couple of strides towards us and gave each of us a hug.

'Comanche warrior welcomes blood brothers,' he said in his mock Native American voice.

'Good to see you, too,' I said. 'Whatever the circumstances may prove to be.'

Bull opened the boot — the trunk, I suppose we had to say now — and we stowed our bergans. We looked at each other and Bull produced a coin. He tossed it in the air. I lost the call and got in the front seat, Bull was grinning as he got in the back and stretched out across the seats.

'Where are we off to?' I asked, hoping it wasn't too far.

'The foothills of the Pecos,' Red said. 'About an hour should do it.'

He kick-shifted the automatic box down a gear and overtook a sedan that was struggling to maintain momentum up a steep incline. I closed my eyes.

I wanted to ask him when he was going to

explain his distress call, but didn't dare risk breaking his concentration.

'If you don't mind waiting,' he said, 'I'll tell you all about why I need you when we get to the ranch. Stan and Pieter arrived last night, but I said to them that I only wanted to go through it once. Too painful to have to cry for help.'

'How are they keeping?' I asked.

'Stan the Man, Stan the Plan, tactician extraordinaire, is already getting the lie of the land and making a list of what we might need. And Pieter, well Pieter, he hasn't got any slimmer. Been living too good a life now that he's got money behind him.'

We'd each split, with our other comrades in arms, ten million euros that we'd taken from the Russians. It worked out at a million each. How they'd spent their share was anybody's guess, but I hoped some of it was frivolously. When you lay your life on the line there needs to be some pleasure. Highs and lows — that was the mercenaries' lot.

The scenery flashed by and the flatness of the plains began to give way to the gradual rise towards the Pecos. It was a long hour.

We drove through a small town which was like a facsimile from Clint Eastwood movies: clapboard fronts to the stores, boardwalk, bar with swinging doors. All it needed was tumbleweed rolling down the street.

'This is O'Haraville,' Red said. 'Well, they might as well call it that. Senator O'Hara owns most of it. Is the mayor, too. And the mayor appoints the sheriff. What he doesn't own, he keeps under his control.'

Red pulled off the country road and on to a dirt track. There was a sign saying 'Lazy Z Ranch'. He stopped so that we could all marvel at the view — surely he'd never get tired of this.

'Wow!' Bull said.

'Yeah, wow,' Red said. 'And it's all mine.'

The track led on through green fields, stretching as far as the eye could see to the left and the right. Up ahead were the jagged peaks of the Pecos. The sun was starting to set and sink down behind the mountains. There was that blue tinge to the red glow of the sky that comes with sunset and it picked out the mountains in sharp relief, making them look as if you could reach out and touch them. Sitting beneath this spectacle was a two-storey wood-framed ranch house, painted a dazzling white, with a large porch running along the front of the building. To the left of the main house was a smaller wooden building, presumably the bunkhouse of old, a barn and a long row of stables.

'This must have cost more than a million,' I

said. 'How did you manage to afford it?'

'I won it in a poker game,' Red said. 'Four queens to his full house.' He sighed. 'Go on, say it. Everyone does.'

'Lucky bastard,' Bull and I said together. 'You bloody lucky bastard.'

'Reckon so,' he said, beaming a huge smile. 'I reckon so.'

3

Stan and Pieter met us with cold beers and we sat on the porch playing catch-up. Red perched himself on the outside rail of the porch and the rest of us leaned back on chairs with the front legs off the floor and our feet on the rail, trying to outcool each other. Pieter, long blond hair slightly receding at the temples, vivid green eyes, looked embarrassed.

'I know what you're thinking,' he said, 'but I wasn't expecting another operation. OK, I've let myself get a bit out of shape, but the weight will soon come off.'

'Not without some hard work,' Bull said. 'We'll start on that in the morning.'

'What have you been doing since we last met?' I asked.

'I now run a safari business. Trips through Kruger. High class, mind. All the trimmings including gourmet food and wine.'

'That makes sense,' I said. 'Been eating the profits?'

'And knowing you,' Bull said, 'they'll be some ladies around, too.'

Pieter was a ladies' man — an incorrigible

womanizer. I'd lost count of the number of fights he'd — we'd — been in with irate husbands or boyfriends.

'Wealthy widows,' he said, smiling. 'What a life.'

'And you, Stan?' I asked.

Stan rocked his chair back a little more and stretched out his long legs to the full. He was wearing sand-coloured chinos with an immaculate crease. His shirt was dark blue and looked like it had just come out of the packaging. His shoes were brown leather and so highly polished you could have used them as a mirror. He produced a crisp white handkerchief to polish his sunglasses. Like always, Stan had covered every detail.

'I have a small hotel with a restaurant on one of our lakes,' he said. 'Good business. I am happy and settled. All I need is a good woman to share my life with, and I'm working on that.'

'Bet you've got a spreadsheet of all the eligible females?'

He blushed. 'Someone's got to look after the detail.'

It was time for the crunch question. I turned towards Red.

'So, Red, what have you got in store for the four of us contented people? Beautiful though this country is, it wouldn't be to admire the sunsets, I guess. What have you got all of us into?'

'It all started a couple of weeks after I moved in. The men — I have about a dozen cowhands here, or did, I should say — all think I'm a jinx. The first thing that happened was that we lost some steers; seems that one of the waterholes had got polluted somehow.'

'Might it have been an accident? I asked. 'Some natural reason? Or do you think it was deliberate?'

'At the time I thought I'd just been unlucky — I was still learning the trade of ranching. Then other things started to occur.'

Slowly our chair legs went back down to the floor and we all leaned forward.

'My cook disappears without trace and without collecting the pay that is due. Then my foreman got injured in a hit and run — might not walk again. Looking back now, I don't think it was an accident, because just a few days later some of the men went into town to let off some steam on pay day and got into a fight — got pretty badly beaten up. The guys who did it — bikers — said they didn't like our sort of people in town.'

'Our sort of people?' Bull asked.

'I presume what he meant by that was my being half Comanche. Can't think what else.'

Bull looked at me. I knew where he was

going. We'd only been here five minutes before meeting one bigot. I raised my hand to still him for a while.

'Did the guy from whom you won the ranch have any problems?'

'The men say no. Just a regular ranch, ticking over nicely.'

'And he was white?' I asked.

'Yeah. Been here a while and never had any trouble.'

'OK. Is that it or is there any more we need to know?'

'One last incident. One of the jeeps we use to get around the place had a blowout on one of its tyres.' He dug into his pocket. 'I heard this rattling around inside when I was trying to mend the puncture.'

He threw something towards me. I caught it. It was a bullet. I rolled it beneath my fingers and assessed the weight. I thought it was Pieter's territory. I passed it to him.

'Hunting rifle,' he said after a brief examination. 'Good for accuracy and packs a punch.'

'And pretty common around here, I guess,' I said.

Red nodded. 'It's what kids are brought up on. Practise on squirrels and such. I'd reckon every home has one.'

'OK,' I said. 'Someone doesn't want you

around. We have to find out who and why.'

'Tell us about Senator O'Hara?' Bull asked.

'He's one of my neighbours. Never met him in person, but seen him on the local TV station a lot. Why do you ask?'

'We had a run in with him at the airport,' I said. 'Called Bull 'boy'.'

'Wow! And did he get away with it?'

'For the time being,' Bull said.

'We need a plan,' I said. 'First, whom and what do we need to protect? Have you got a map of this area showing your ranch and the neighbouring countryside?

'There's one in the car,' said Red. 'You guys go inside and we'll continue talking while we eat. I'll be right back.'

We moved through a swing door and into a large living area. There was a pine table at one end that could seat a dozen hungry cowhands, at the other end of the room were a lot of armchairs and sofas, mostly old and worn.

'Your inheritance from the previous owner, I presume?' I said to Red when he arrived back from getting the map.

'Signs of a bad poker player,' he said. 'Never enough left to spend on life's little luxuries.'

'Reckon so,' I said, nodding.

'The cook's Chinese and she has made us a

chilli,' Stan said. 'By the smell of it I need to give her some lessons in Western cooking.'

Someone, presumably the meticulous Stan, had laid the table with plates, cutlery and napkins, salt, pepper, crackers in the American style and various ketchups and sauces. There were water and wine glasses, beers and a couple of bottles of Californian Cabernet Sauvignon. Red made a space and spread the map out. We sat down and waited while the cook brought in a large bowl of chilli con carne and followed that with one of rice. She was an attractive, small, slim girl; Chinese, from the south of the country by the look of her eyes and the absence of the heavy Mongol features of the north. Looked like she needed a good meal, which didn't bode well for her culinary skills.

'This is Ho,' Stan said, nodding at the girl.

'Hi, Ho,' said Pieter, laughing.

'Thank you for very original greeting,' she said, sighing.

Pieter gave her his winning smile. 'Maybe I can teach you some tricks of the trade,' he said.

'I've already got that covered,' said Stan defensively. 'Things are going to change around here.'

'Well, if you need my help, you know where to come,' Pieter said to the girl.

'That will not be necessary,' Stan said, a little too quickly.

Ho put her hands together and bowed. She turned and left the room, Stan and Pieter watching her closely. I could smell trouble brewing. Made a mental note to rein in Pieter. I didn't want any fighting in the ranks.

The bowls circulated round the table as we helped ourselves. I took a mouthful. My tongue exploded — this was seriously hot. So much so that it might have been declared a biological weapon by any government that needed an excuse to go to war. A glance round the table told me everyone else felt the same. The ranch hands can't have liked it — I wouldn't blame them if more left.

'These are the Pecos mountains,' Red said, pushing his plate away and pointing to a dark jagged line on the map. 'My land runs up to the edge. Land's not good for much at the foothills: too dry with all the rain coming down on the other side, but there's good grazing on the plains.' He got out a pen and drew a square on the map. 'This is my spread. And adjoining me on the left is Senator O'Hara's land. Much like mine — mostly suited for raising cattle.'

'Put this in perspective,' I said. 'How big is it? How long to get from one side to another?'

'We usually take the jeeps, although

sometimes I ride one of the horses,' — Red used to scratch a living by riding in rodeos — 'and, I suppose, it would take about ten minutes to go round the perimeter.'

'Ten minutes can be a long time when you're waiting for the cavalry to arrive,' Stan said.

Red drew two rectangles on the right, one above the other. He pointed to the top one and said, 'This is the Blenkensteins' land — they've been here a long time, so I understand. Probably in their sixties, maybe seventies by now.'

'And this?' I pointed to the lower rectangle.

'That's the Alamo Retreat.'

Bull and I looked at each other and raised our eyebrows. Red caught the look.

'Explain, please?' he said.

'We ran into them at the airport, too. Young woman called Fey and two teenage girls, Cameron and Lucy. Seemed harmless enough, although a little unconventional.'

'It's a sort of commune,' Red said. 'Self-supporting, live off the land, back to the garden, as they said for Woodstock. They're vegetarians, so they plant crops rather than raising cattle. Fey came here once when I'd first moved in. Brought a cake as a welcome present and used it as an excuse to try to save my soul. Saw it was a losing battle and I've not seen her since.'

'What are our resources?' I asked Red.

Stan got up from the table and went across to the far side of the room where the light was poor and it was hard to see what he was carrying. When he returned, he dumped his load on the table and started to distribute it.

'Red and I spent the day in town yesterday. Mobiles for all of us.'

He slid them across the table to each of us in turn.

'Already programmed with all our numbers.'

Then the juicy stuff was dealt out.

'Brownings for the four of us and a Magnum for Red.'

'You're not still using a Magnum, are you?' Bull said. 'Too few bullets for my liking.'

'I only aim to need one,' Red said.

'Touché,' said Bull.

'And you'll be taking a shotgun, too?' I said.

Red's eyesight wasn't as good as in the old days. Even with his glasses it was more reassuring to know that Red could scatter the pellets anywhere and everywhere and didn't need to aim straight in an emergency. We all had to rely on each other and that meant taking no chances.

'Yeah,' Red said. 'It worked well last time. Worth sticking to.'

Stan went round the table dishing out pieces of paper.

'Gun permits for each of us. Make sure you sign them and carry them around all the time. Red says that the local sheriff is a tyrant. There's shoulder holsters for each of us, although in this hot weather we won't want to be wearing jackets. Best to just tuck it in your waistband at the back.'

'Tomorrow we spend the morning getting to know the territory,' I said. Turning to Red, I asked, 'How many cowhands have you got and could we rely on any help from them?'

'I'm down to just eight — hard to work the ranch with so few. They're all drifters. They're staying in the bunkhouse — bed and board is part of their pay. If it came down to it, I wouldn't like to rely on them for help.'

'Sleeping arrangements?'

'There's room for you all here, if you don't mind sharing.'

'I'll take the bunkhouse,' I said.

'Me, too,' said Bull.

'Let's turn in and start early tomorrow.'

'Thanks, guys,' Red said, smiling. 'I feel better already. Whatever they throw at us, we can handle it. Let them come on, I say.'

Bull and I picked up our bergans. 'You better introduce us to the crew,' I said to Red. 'Just in case they're a bit jumpy.'

He led the way across a yard and round behind the house. There was a single-storey building with a tin roof. I hoped it wouldn't rain — must sound like hell inside the bunkhouse. Red opened the door and went inside. There were two rows of bunks one up, one down — five along each side of the room. A single ceiling-light gave an insufficient glow. I could make out that some of the beds were already occupied. Faces turned towards us.

'Hi, guys,' Red said. 'Some friends have come to help. You'll have the pleasure of their company during their stay. Make 'em welcome. See you all in the morning.'

The reception wasn't exactly rapturous. Still, maybe they didn't take too kindly to strangers here.

They looked across at a heavily built guy with long brown hair and a scar across his cheek. Boss man, I guessed.

'You gonna sort things out?' he asked.

'You bet,' I said.

'Well you can start with the food. I like Chinese food as much as the next man — '

'I'm the next man,' cut in a small weasel-faced man, 'and I hate Chinese food.'

'Shut up,' the big man said. He turned to me. 'Food's not good enough for working men. Sort it out.'

'We'll do what we can,' I said.

'That's our philosophy in a nutshell,' Bull said.

The big man nodded, then frowned as he took a moment to work out what Bull had said. 'You take the bunks near the door,' he said.

Furthest from the stove and nearest the draught from the door. We didn't argue. We had to earn their respect and there was only one way to do that. Best not to fight among ourselves.

I turned to Bull.

'Up or down? I said.

'Down.'

'First or second?'

'I'll take first shift,' he said, placing his gun on the pillow. 'I'll wake you in two hours.'

'Welcome to Texas,' I said, kicking off my shoes and climbing up to the top bunk. 'Sleep well. But only during my shift.'

'Reckon so,' he said.

* * *

It was now my shift. Someone was snoring at the far end of the bunkhouse and it was starting to get on my nerves. I pressed the button on my watch and the light told me it was three o'clock. I thought I heard a shuffling sound outside. The door burst open and rocked back on its hinges. There was a slapping sound of something hitting the floor. I put on the light and reeled back. The floor was crawling with snakes.

I grabbed my gun and started to fire.

Bull awoke and instinctively drew his gun.

'You take the left,' I said to Bull.

I fired and Bull shot a moment after. Someone screamed. Panic started to break out.

'Don't move,' I shouted. 'Stay exactly where you are.'

We were aiming at the heads of the snakes — rattlers, going by the erect tails and the chilling sound that was coming from them. I reckoned there were about a dozen. Good target practice.

Because it was cold and night-time, the snakes moved slowly. Easy pickings. A couple of minutes of rapid fire from Bull and me and it was all over. The bunkhouse floor was littered with snake blood and corpses, some still wriggling as their nervous systems began to shut down. Bull and I let out breaths simultaneously.

'You know what this means?' I said.

'We're going to have to put someone to watch outside.'

'Stan will do a rota,' I said.

The door burst open again and Red, Stan and Pieter entered with guns out.

'What the hell?' said Red.

'Someone wanted to give us a biology lesson,' I said. From the look on the faces of the ranch hands it had been pretty effective, too. I turned to address the men. 'Now you've seen what we can do,' I said. 'You can rest easy. We'll protect you. Someone get a broom and clear up this mess. The rest of you try to get back to sleep, you've work to do in the morning. Everything's going to be normal.'

'Does that mean the usual Chinese breakfast?' the big man said as he climbed into his bunk.

'Reckon so,' I said.

'Shit,' he said, pulling the covers over him. 'Make sure someone dumps those snakes where the cook can't get at them. I don't want her getting any ideas for a special banquet.'

The five of us left the room and went back to the ranch house. Ho, roused by the gunfire, had made a pot of coffee. She set it on the table along with half a dozen mugs, gathered her nightdress around her, bowed and left. I grabbed some spare blankets from one of the bedrooms and readied myself for another couple of hours on watch on the porch.

'I'll take first shift,' said Stan. 'I've got

things to mull over and lists to make.'

'At least we know one thing,' I said. 'Red's not exaggerating. Someone wants him out of here. I think this is escalation. Like we said, 'who and why' and what the hell has he got in store for us next?'

Stan took the blankets I'd got and went outside. Red lit a fire. We stood around drinking coffee, savouring the warmth of it and the fire, and staring into the flames as if they were going to provide the answers to our question.

'We know one thing,' said Bull. 'Whoever did this has a vivid imagination.'

'Makes him even more dangerous,' I said. 'Hard to predict his next move.'

'At least we know one other thing,' Bull said. 'We can still do it. Shooting the heads off snakes was a great test and we passed it.'

'Going to make the ranch hands jittery,' I said.

'More jittery, you mean,' said Red. 'What are we going to do?'

'Stay alert,' I said. 'Make sure we don't get caught out next time. Whatever's in store for us. Now we know the lengths to which someone will go to force Red to leave.'

'Somehow I don't find that very reassuring,' said Pieter. 'It's only going to get worse, isn't it?'

'Reckon so,' I said. 'Only one thing to do.'

'Which is?' said Bull

'Go on the offensive. Take the fight to them.'

'And how are we going to do that?' Red asked.

'I haven't actually worked that bit out yet,' I said.

'Hell,' Bull said. 'I was getting confident there for a moment and then you had to go and spoil it.'

'First things first. We're going to follow Napoleon's words.'

'What doesn't kill me makes me stronger?'

'Nietzsche.'

'*Gesundheit*,' said Red.

'Give me generals who are lucky?' Bull suggested.

'That, too,' I said. 'But I was thinking of 'an army marches on its stomach'.'

'Good to have a long-term plan,' said Bull. 'What do we do after breakfast?'

'Come up with another plan, of course,' I said.

'Of course,' Bull said. 'Now why didn't I think of that?'

'Takes a special talent,' I said.

Bull gave a grin and shook his head.

'White man speak with forked tongue,' said Red.

'It was ever thus,' said Bull.

4

Pieter was still rubbing a couple of hours' sleep from his eyes when Bull dragged him from the ranch house into the cool crisp air of the early morning. We'd agreed he would put on a show, something to raise the ranch hands' spirits and take their minds off the events of the night before.

Bull and Pieter got down on the timber deck of the porch and, with Bull acting as if he was a sergeant-major in the army trying to break a new recruit, started doing press-ups. Bull quickly established a steady rhythm and Pieter tried to keep up as best he could. There was another reason for that, apart from making the effort to get into shape. He had an audience — didn't want to be embarrassed. The ranch hands came out from breakfast and stood there watching. The heavily built guy we'd seen the previous night tilted his head back and gave a snigger. He got down beside Bull.

'Ten bucks on Jesse,' someone said.

'I'll be willing to take your money,' I said.

Wallets were opened and dollar bills were brought out.

Bull barely looked up, just kept on going.

Although he had already done about thirty press-ups before Jesse started, I reckoned my money was safe. Bull could keep this up all day if needed.

Jesse matched him and looked like he was feeling pleased with himself. When the count had reached forty, Bull looked across at Jesse and smiled. Then he took one hand off the ground and continued to push himself up and ease himself down.

'Shit,' said one of the onlookers.

Jesse crumpled, knowing there was no way he could beat Bull, feeling the fight go out of him. He stood up and nodded sagely. 'Welcome to the Lazy Z,' he said and stretched out his hand. Bull sprung up and shook it. 'A word of warning,' Jesse said. 'Don't eat the breakfast.'

'Thanks for the tip,' Bull said.

'Where are you guys from?' Jesse asked.

'Pieter's from South Africa,' Bull said. 'Stan's from Poland and Johnny and I are from a little island in the Caribbean called St Jude. Be good to wrap this up and get back to our families.'

'Be good to have a family,' Jesse said. 'We're all drifters. Some day it would be nice to settle down with a little place of my own. Trouble is, I always seem to blow my pay each week. There's a hell of a cathouse in town.'

The rest of the hands who had been listening mumbled their agreement.

We went inside for breakfast. Jesse had been right. What wasn't burnt was undercooked, and there was so much fat you could have greased train axles. Stan was going to have his work cut out with this cook; pretty though she was, that wasn't going to save her from the wrath of a bunch of very hungry men. As we had said earlier, an army marches on its stomach — what you don't want to do is clutch it all the time, groaning in pain.

We drank coffee and the others listened to my plan of action for the day.

'We need to scout out the territory,' I said. 'Find the vulnerable points and places where we can put a good defence. Bull, you and Pieter take one of the jeeps and study the west side. Red and I will take horses and cover the east. Stan, give this cook some lessons and fast. We'll meet up here in a couple of hours and compare notes. Then we prepare for tonight.'

'What are we doing then?' Red asked.

'You're going to pay your hands a bonus and we're all going into town to celebrate.'

'Shake the tree and see what falls down?' Bull said.

'Exactly,' I said. 'Red, we need to spread the word. Get one of your hands to go to town to buy something and let them know it's celebration night. We need to persuade the enemy — whoever he is — to organize a reception committee.'

'I'll give you a list of food to buy,' said Stan. 'If I'm going to teach the cook a few tricks, I'll need some raw materials. Steaks tonight, everybody?'

'Seems like the appropriate thing to do,' said Pieter, 'seeing that we're on a cattle ranch.'

'OK, let's saddle up and get going before the worst of the heat arrives,' I said. 'Oh, and take the handguns. Better safe than sorry.'

* * *

'I've got just the horse for you,' Red said.

My heart sank. That statement was usually the prelude to being introduced to a horse called Diablo or Beelzebub that no one had been able to break.

The stables had a dozen stalls, six on each side, and a large tack area at the front. Red opened the gate on one stable and led out a big grey stallion. The horse was a magnificent beast, sixteen hands high at least, and seemed to handle well.

'Why just for me?' I asked.

'Don't you know your Bible? Revelations. 'And I looked, and behold a pale horse: and his name that sat on him was Death, and Hell followed with him.''

'Is that how you see me?'

'Well, what normally happens when you get involved with something?'

I shook my head. Maybe he was right. Certainly the Russian must have felt that way when I shot him in the head, spraying brains and blood all over Anna.

'I don't do it on purpose, you know.'

'Nothing to apologize for. The deaths have all been among the opposition. You only kill to protect someone else. I wonder who the next in line will be? Anyway,' he said, 'let's saddle up and get going before the heat builds too much.'

'Bull and I are used to heat,' I said. 'But on St Jude it is a dry heat, ideal, eminently bearable. Here the air is laden with moisture, damp, humid, generally uncomfortable.'

'Comes from the hills,' Red said, 'and the clouds generated there. You'll get used to it.'

He found a saddle, harness, reins and all the other paraphernalia and passed them to me. 'His name is Shadow. You'll have to ride him Western style — one-handed.'

I walked over to Shadow and patted his

head. He nuzzled into me and suddenly I knew that this was a good horse and that we would bond together. I placed the blanket across his back and started to prepare him for the ride.

'Got your gun?' Red asked.

I nodded. 'And you?'

'The Magnum is in my waistband. The shotgun will go in the pouch on the saddle. Bring it on.'

I put the Browning in the shoulder holster and looped it securely around the pommel of the saddle. Then we set out like two cowboys from more than a century before. We headed northwards towards the mountains and our plan was to work our way along the northern and eastern boundaries of Red's land and back to the ranch.

It took a while to get used to the one-handed style of riding, but Shadow was very responsive and almost led me rather than the other way round. I knew my muscles would make me pay for this tomorrow, but it was worth it. It was good to be back in the saddle again.

'Where did you learn to ride?' Red asked.

'England. When I was a teenager. It was my mother's way to get me out of the house when my father was around.'

'Lucky for your father,' he said.

We trotted on and after about ten minutes came to a waterhole fed by a large stream running swiftly down from the mountains.

'This is where the water was poisoned,' Red said.

I looked around and up to the foothills.

'Not much of a plan,' I said. 'With the fast flow of the stream, the water would have cleared pretty quickly.' I shook my head. 'This was a warning, not an attempt to wipe out the herd.'

'But why?' he said. 'Why do they want me out of here? That's what I can't see.'

'We'll work it out. Maybe we'll have some luck in town tonight. Mouths loosened by drink or the threat of a broken arm.'

We rode on. It was truly God's own country. The plains were lush and spread as far as the eye could see until they merged into the foothills of the Pecos. One problem: it was going to be hard to defend. Too big, too open, too easy for someone to come through the boundaries to the left and right or make their way across the foothills and down.

When we climbed the lower reaches of the hills, the horses nimbly picking their way, we could see a ramshackle farmhouse in the distance.

'That's the Blenkensteins' land,' Red said. 'They haven't got as big a spread as I have.

Much harder for them to make a living.'

'Well pay them a call tomorrow. See if they've had similar problems to you.'

'In some ways that would be comforting. Not just me as a target.'

We turned due south and rode along the eastern border. After around an hour we came to the boundary between the Blenkensteins's land and that of the Alamo retreat. We were both deep in thought when the call came.

'Hi, neighbour.'

'Oh God,' Red said. 'It's the girl from the Retreat. She'll try to convert us both.'

As she came closer I could see that it was Fey. Her hair was loose and rippled in the breeze. She was wearing blue jeans — de rigueur, I imagined, in this cowboy country — and a shirt knotted below her breasts so that we could see her bare midriff. She was riding a palomino. Bareback! And I had thought I was a good rider.

The two girls were with her, riding ponies; Cameron was on a chestnut mare and Lucy on a bay stallion. They were also riding bareback. That made me feel even more inadequate. They made their way over to the boundary fence.

'A fine morning,' said Fey. Then she turned to face me and became pensive. 'Didn't we meet at the airport?'

'It was my pleasure,' I said.

'Ma'am,' Red said, taking off his hat and doffing it to her.

'Good to see you again, Red,' she said. 'How was the pie?'

'Just like Grandma used to make.'

I looked across at him. 'Just like Grandma used to make?'

'Comanches got to eat pie, too. Not just the preserve of the white man, you know. Wouldn't be surprised if the Comanche didn't invent the pie.'

I was just about to laugh when it happened. Because light travels faster than sound I saw the fence post to my right splinter. A split second later I heard the sound of the shot. Lucy's pony was spooked, bucked and set off like the wind towards the hills. Lucy hung on to the mane for dear life, but was bouncing up and down and rolling from side to side. It was only a matter of time before she was thrown off and goodness knows what damage would be caused; broken bones might be the least of the injuries: she wasn't wearing a helmet.

I turned Shadow around and rode back from the fence, yanked the reins sharply to the left, took a run up and kicked with my heels. Shadow jumped the fence cleanly. I immediately headed on a course that would take me to the right of Lucy and keep the fence on her left. I had to try to pen her in.

Lucy switched her grip from the mane to around the pony's neck, her back arching up and her bottom clear of the pony's loins, her knees were nowhere close to its flanks — control was pretty much zero.

The pony was swift, but no match for Shadow. I drew alongside and gradually came near enough to take the harness and pull sharply backwards. The pony bucked, but wouldn't respond to me. It kept going on towards the hills and the boundary fence of the Blenkensteins' land. If I couldn't make the pony stop, I only had one option.

I slowed Shadow down until I was level with Lucy, leaned across and took her by the waist. I hauled her from the pony's back and swung her ahead of me on to Shadow. I breathed a sigh of relief and slowed down. Lucy looked at me and, the danger registering, the relief settling in, began to cry. I pulled her close and set Shadow on a course back to where Red, Fey and Cameron had dismounted, using the horses for cover against another bullet. Maybe there was something to this Western-style riding after all: I couldn't have brought off such a manoeuvre with both of my hands on the reins.

I swung Lucy down from the saddle; she ran over to Fey and fell into her arms.

'Nice work,' Red said. 'With riding like that I might make you an honorary Comanche. Heap big warrior brave.'

Lucy started to calm down and came across to me. 'Thank you,' she said. 'What's your name?'

'Johnny,' I said. 'Johnny Silver.'

'We would like to find a way to repay you, Mr Silver. Would you come for dinner tomorrow night?'

'I'd be delighted,' I said. 'And now I think it's time you all went back to your retreat. We don't know how safe it is here any more. The pony will find its way back.'

'Till tomorrow then,' Fey said, lifting Lucy up on the back of the palomino and climbing up behind her. 'Seven o'clock. Bring Red and the other man who was at the airport.'

They turned and rode slowly south-east. I lined Shadow up and, with much more confidence this time, jumped to Red's side of the fence.

'Whoever fired,' Red said, 'it was lucky for us he was such a bad shot.'

'Or a very good one,' I said.

5

We were lined up again on the porch, eating sandwiches with Stan's beloved dill pickles and drinking cold beer. No one was trying to outcool anyone else. The time for posturing was over — it was serious now.

Bull took a sip of beer and winced.

'Something the matter?' I said.

'Beer tastes funny,' he said. 'I'll go and get another.'

'Plenty in the ice bucket,' I said.

'It's OK,' he said, getting up. 'I think I'll have a warm one.'

'A warm beer?' I said, surprised. 'Who in the world drinks warm beer?'

'I do,' he said. 'Want to make something of it?'

I shrugged. Friction in the camp. Time to back off and analyse the situation. 'Go ahead,' I said. 'It's a free country.'

He went inside and reappeared with a can of beer. Took a sip. I swear I saw him shudder. Something to investigate here.

'Observations, gentlemen,' I said. 'What have we learned from this morning's reconnaissance?'

'Hell of a place to defend,' Bull said. 'Damn sniper in the hills could pick anybody off real easy.'

'Then *we* will have to hold the hills,' I said. 'We'll have to take turns on watch. Red, can you get us a sniper rifle? A Barrett M82A1 would be best.'

It was my favourite sniper rifle — effective range of 1000 metres and could put a hole in a tank.

'We could go to the gun shop this afternoon. See what he's got.'

I nodded. 'What else?' I asked Bull and Pieter.

'The fences wouldn't deter any one,' Bull said. 'High enough to keep cattle in, but not so tall that a man couldn't climb easily.'

'It's all so big,' said Pieter. 'Takes too long to get from one side to the other, or from here to the furthest point on the foothills. I suppose we could parcel it up into more manageable units and have one man on each.'

'Split our forces?' I said. 'Having us as a combined unit is our strength. We don't want to give up that advantage unless we absolutely have to.'

I pondered on the best defensive position and couldn't find an obvious answer.

'I see you've been busy, Stan,' I said, looking at the cross of gaffer tape marking one side of the porch.

'I've laid out a few firing positions,' he said in his most serious voice — which wasn't much different from his normal voice. 'I concentrated on inside the house and on various points surrounding it.' He shook his head and gave us his usual melancholy face 'Tricky, though.'

I raised an eyebrow in a questioning look.

'No clear field of fire,' he said. 'Bunkhouse gets in the way here at the front, and the stable masks the view to the back. I've done the best we can, but again it means splitting up. I'd feel much safer if we could have all stayed in the house — one man guarding each side. That will have to be the last line of defence.'

'Now you can see why I needed help,' Red said. 'One man's a sitting duck.'

'Not much better with five,' I said.

'Reckon so,' Red said. 'Sorry to drag you all along.'

'No need for apologies,' I said. 'One for all and all for one.'

'So tell us what happened on your reconnoitre, d'Artagnan,' Bull said.

I relayed the action of the morning and our supposed lucky escape.

'I think the shooter missed deliberately,' I said. 'Whatever game someone is playing, I think we're still in the early stages. Up till now everything — including that gunshot — has been a warning. Whoever's behind it is hoping we'll quit.'

'And we won't,' Bull said. 'He don't know you.'

'Reckon so,' I said. 'We're not going to run.'

'Not yet,' said Stan, bringing a touch of reality to the bravado. 'I like to know what I'm running from.'

* * *

Red, Stan and I drove into town. Stan was there partly as our armourer and also because he had to get some steaks and side orders to feed everybody before the evening's fun.

The gun shop was dark inside, as though trying to provide a hiding-place from the relentless heat of the sun. There were glass display counters for handguns and racks along the walls with rifles, shotguns and other large weapons. The storekeeper was a small man with glasses and a receding hairline. He had on a blue-and-white-striped apron and looked like a chef who'd forgotten his hat. The apron was covered not with stains from food, but with oil from where he had cleaned the guns.

'Barrett, you say,' he said, sucking at his teeth. 'Now let me see.'

He gazed along the walls and then nodded his head. He picked a rifle out of a rack and handed it to me.

'Can't do no Barrett,' he said. 'Got a Dragonov, though.'

I handed the gun to Stan. He started to break it down, laying the parts on one of the counters. When he had finished, he inspected each part in minute detail.

'Got a good range,' the storekeeper said.

'Eight hundred metres,' Stan said. 'Muzzle velocity eight hundred and thirty metres per second. Not as good as the Barrett, but it will do.' He started to reassemble the gun. 'Need a couple of boxes of shells, too.'

The storekeeper dug around under one of the counters and came up with some boxes. He laid them on the glass counter top, took a pad out of his apron pocket and wrote down some figures. He tore off the top sheet and passed it to Red.

Red stared at it.

'You could always try elsewhere,' the storekeeper said.

Red peeled off a wad of notes and handed it to the storekeeper.

'Good day, gentlemen,' the man said with an insincere smile.

Stan picked up the rifle and the boxes of shells and we stepped outside into a furnace so filled with water vapour that you could have taken a handful and squeezed the water from it. Waiting for us was the bulk of the local sheriff.

He was a large man — sixteen or seventeen stone, maybe — with a face that was tanned by the sun and reddened by the wind that blew down from the mountains. Along his forehead was a frown that looked like it had been tattooed there in order to save him the trouble of using his muscles. He was dressed in faded chinos with an iron crease and a blue shirt, similarly pressed. The badge was pinned to the pocket of the shirt. The whole ensemble was finished off by a gunbelt with a Colt Magnum sticking out.

'Howdy, Red,' he said, taking in the three of us and the rifle. 'Planning a little shooting practice?'

'Squirrels,' Red said.

'Mighty big squirrels if you need a rifle that size,' the sheriff said. 'Be kind enough to step into my office, boys.'

He led the way along the sidewalk to a small building with a white door. He pushed it open and ushered us inside.

The air conditioning was running at its maximum setting and you could almost hear the sheriff sigh as he stepped into the cool. A deputy sat reading a paper. As we entered he took his feet off the desk and returned them to the floor. He nodded at us and went back to his paper.

The sheriff sat down at a shiny-topped steel-framed desk with a name plate perched on top: Sheriff Tucker, it said. He looked up at us.

'Can I see your gun permits, boys?' he said. 'To cover the rifle and the guns you've got tucked down your waistbands.'

Much to his disappointment, I presumed, we handed over the permits. I was getting the feeling that this was not a friendly town. The sheriff handed back the permits and looked me in the eye.

'You're not from around here, are you?' he said

'Does the smile betray me?'

He frowned.

'I have to warn you,' he said, 'this is a wise-guy-free town and I want to keep it that way. No lip and no trouble. Do I make myself clear?'

'Reckon so,' I said. 'Trouble is the last thing we want. But if it comes along, we aim to handle it. You can spread that round on your travels.'

He gave a sigh. 'You're British,' he said

with a look that suggested he should have been speaking more slowly.

'English, actually,' I replied.

'*Actually*,' he said. 'Don't get much *actually* round here. Now you take your *actually* ass out of my *actually* office and, if you know what's good for you, out of my *actually* town.'

'Nice meeting you, Sheriff,' I said. I nodded to Red and we turned around and headed for the door. The deputy was still reading the cartoons in the newspaper. Good to have reliable back-up if you're ever in a tight spot. Maybe that accounted for the sheriff's tough-guy impressions. Time would tell.

⋆ ⋆ ⋆

The three of us walked the main street and got our bearings for the evening visit. There was a hotel with a porch and an old black man in a dark-blue uniform in a rocking chair with a grey-muzzled dog sitting by his side. The dog was panting, even though he was in the shade. The black man just kept rocking as if he could take whatever heat God sent down.

I left Red and Stan to carry on the tour and went up to the porch of the hotel.

'Where can a guy get a beer around here?' I asked him.

With an economy of movement he raised his thumb and gestured backwards inside the hotel. I went in and found a small bar area just off the reception. I bought two beers and took them out to the porch. I handed one to the old man and stretched down to stroke the dog. He opened a mouth that was missing several teeth and licked my hand.

'Good sign,' the old man said. 'If he didn't like you, he could have gummed you to death.'

'A good dog is hard to find,' I said.

'Easier than finding a good man.'

'Reckon so.'

I sat down on the porch rail and looked down at the old man.

'See you made acquaintance with the sheriff,' he said.

'You must see a lot from here. Tell me about him.'

'Sheriff Tucker? Bark's worse than his bite. Anyways, whenever there's trouble, he never seems to be around. Good nose for trouble, has Tucker. Still, it's a quiet town, or at least it was till Red showed up. Been a storm brewing for a while now. Pretty soon it's gonna break.'

'But why? What has Red done to cause a fuss?'

'Maybe 'cos he's half-Indian. The senator

likes his town white as the snow in wintertime.'

I went inside to think it over. I got another two beers and a bowl of peanuts and went back outside. I took a handful of peanuts and gave the bowl and a beer to the old man. I tossed a peanut towards the dog and he caught it mid-air. Still got a trick or two.

I placed the cold bottle against my forehead and then took a long pull. The heat and humidity seemed relentless, even in the shade of the porch. Didn't seem to bother the old man. Maybe if you were here long enough you got used to it.

'What do you know about the Alamo Retreat?' I asked.

'Bunch of long-haired kids. Throwback to the sixties — peace and love and all that. Don't do no harm, although the senator would like to get rid of them, too.'

'Don't seem that tolerant, your senator.

'His daddy was the same and his grandpa, too. Living as if it's the nineteenth century. Don't realize that times have changed.'

'And what about you, old man. What does he think of you?'

'I'm the token black,' he said. 'Been fetching and carrying for this hotel for a whiles now. The senator leaves me alone if I know my place. Calls me boy. Gives me a dollar if I open the door for him.' He shook his head and smiled. 'Boy!'

'Seems like the town should be called Bigotsville.'

'You got it,' he said.

'What about the Blenkensteins?' I asked. 'See much of them?'

'Keep pretty much to themselves. Come to town once a month or so for stores and that's it. Don't eat here, don't drink here. All their money goes to the upkeep of that farm of theirs. Life can be hard for a farmer.'

What's your name, old man?'

'People call me Jerome.'

'Stick around tonight, Jerome. Might be some excitement for you to watch.'

⋆ ⋆ ⋆

When we got back, Stan and Red unloaded the jeep and started to lug the heavy bags of groceries inside. I carried the Dragonov sniper rifle and the two boxes of shells — got to be some perks for being in charge. I went across to the bunk-house and found the men washing and sprucing themselves up ready for their meal and the treat of a night on the town. Jesse, barechested, came up to me.

'What's the plan?' he asked, pulling on a red-checked shirt that was usually the province of lumberjacks.

'Leave at nine,' I said. 'We'll be there before you. Don't acknowledge us.'

'Anything else?' he asked.

'Keep cool. Whatever goes down,' I said with a reassuring smile. 'And stick around and watch the fun.'

He nodded and went back to join the others.

In the house Stan was talking to Ho. 'I need to teach her a few things about Western cooking,' he said to me. 'Why don't you guys relax and I'll join you on the porch in a little while.'

Pieter filled a bucket with ice, put some cans of beer inside and we went out to the porch to think over how we were going to play the evening. Bull joined us with a lowball glass with a light-brown liquid inside.

'What's that?' I asked.

'Bourbon and branchwater,' he said. 'Trying to camouflage myself as a local.'

'And no ice?' I said, seeing a pattern. 'You've got toothache, haven't you?'

'Maybe,' he said.

'You should see a dentist and get it fixed,' I said.

'Dentist in town is good,' Red added.

'Reckon it will go away with time,' Bull said.

'You're scared,' I said, amazed. 'Scared of the dentist. A big guy like you who can shoot the heads off snakes and you're scared of the dentist.'

'I ain't scared of nuttin.'

'Your roots are showing,' I said.

'What?' said Bull.

'Nuttin?'

'Leave it,' Bull said.

I gave a little laugh and shook my head. Just as long as it wasn't a distraction when the doodly-squat hit the fan. Leave it be for a while and see what developed.

We decided to go in two jeeps, park a hundred yards away from the bar and approach separately. The big decision was whether we all went or left someone behind to keep watch. Nobody wanted to miss out on the action. There was one of the ranch hands whose religious beliefs didn't run to bars and cathouses, so we left him as lookout with one of our mobile phones in case he needed to recall us.

We sipped beer and watched the ranch hands come and go for their dinner. They left with smiles on their faces. A good sign, but we went indoors to test the quality of the food for ourselves.

Stan had done well, although, as he later said, you can't go far wrong with steak, chips and salad. The steaks were succulent, the chips crispy, the salad — well, the salad was salad and, purportedly, good for us. We drank just water, keeping ourselves alert for the remainder of the evening. At 8.30 we set off and filtered into the bar one by one at five-minute intervals.

The bar was called La Cantina and was Mexican themed. There were sombreros and pottery flasks hanging from the walls and a big display of different tequilas, only some with worms, behind a long highly polished wooden counter that the barmen could slide drinks along. Guitar music was playing softly in the background. There were about twenty round wooden tables, each seating four people, and two rectangular tables big enough for six. There was a scattering of customers, mostly men. None of them looked threatening. I ordered an orange juice, picked up a local paper and chose a table in the corner where I could look over the top of the paper and see the door.

Bull arrived and took a position in the opposite corner. Red, Stan and Pieter came in one after the other and chose tables with their backs to the wall. At nine o'clock precisely, the ranch hands and Ho walked through the door. They ordered beers, a white wine for Ho and pulled the two rectangular tables together. The barman made a call on his mobile and it seemed a fair bet that the game was on.

Fifteen minutes later seven men walked in. They were big, a little heavy around the middle perhaps, but easily the right size to knock you out with one punch. One was especially big, not so much built like a house but like a whole mansion. He was toned and would be the one to watch in a fight. They were all wearing faded denim jeans, white T-shirts and black leather jackets. The jackets were partly unzipped — not a good sign. On the back of the jackets was a skull motif. Their hair was long and had that greasy sheen that infrequent washing produces; one was grey-haired and seemed to be in charge. They didn't bother ordering drinks. Just walked up to the ranch hands and circled them.

'How'd you like rattlers,' the one with the grey hair said, laughing.

'Ho's gonna cook us up a meal from them,' Jesse said. 'Thanks for that.'

'I thought we made it clear you're not welcome here,' the grey-haired one said. 'Have we got to teach you another lesson?'

'Better include me in that,' I said, getting up.

'Keep your mouth shut and mind your own business,' the grey-haired man said.

'It is my business,' I said. 'If you know what's good for you, you'll back off and walk out through the door while you can.'

The grey-haired man laughed. He probably thought that only Jesse of the ranch hands would be any sort of threat in a fight; if they had to take on one more, then the odds were still well in their favour, especially with Mr Mansion on their side.

'It's my business, too,' Bull said, standing up and showing them six foot six of muscle.

The grey-haired man didn't look so confident now. I didn't think he'd have the sense to walk away. They had come to do a job and they couldn't back down now without losing a lot of face and the dream of making some easy money.

The grey-haired man dispatched Mr Mansion and one other of his crew towards Bull and only one to me; I was offended.

Red stood up. Then Pieter and finally Stan, who both walked across the room so that they had their backs to the counter and we effectively surrounded them rather than vice versa.

The grey-haired man walked up to Pieter, sensing he would be the easiest target. He swung a punch that Pieter swerved away from and threw a straight left in return. The grey-haired man staggered and took a step back, rubbing his chin. He approached Pieter again, this time more warily. He pulled a length of bicycle chain from the back pocket of his jeans and swung it around.

'OK, guys,' I said. 'They didn't heed the warning. Time to show them what you get if you're foolish.'

I came nearer to the man appointed to me and feinted with my right, making him take a step backwards. He picked up a beer glass from a nearby table and smashed it. The jagged edge he thrust at me.

Then all hell broke out. Jesse joined in to even up the numbers and there were fights taking place everywhere. Even Ho got involved. She was startling: producing karate high kicks and chops that had a force belying her slight frame. I wished I could have stopped to watch her, but that was not to be the case. Bull and Mansion were locked in a serious duel where neither had the advantage nor would back away. Tables were broken by flying bodies landing on them, chairs were thrown across the room and the bikers all had some sort of weapon — bottles, knuckle-dusters, knives. This was serious now.

I backed off from the guy with the broken glass. He took a step closer and thrust it at my head. I grabbed his right arm, pulled him towards me and swept my right leg across the back of his. He couldn't hold his balance and I helped him fall forward by chopping him on the back of his neck. He got up slowly and approached me again. He was ready for me to repeat the move. Instead I punched him hard in the stomach with my right fist and, as he buckled, I hit him on the chin for good measure. He jackknifed back and landed in a heap on the floor. He crawled away and that was when I saw the movement. His hand went inside his jacket and came out with a gun.

I fired twice. The first bullet hit the gun and took it out of his hand. The second drilled a hole through his palm. He screamed and the fight went out of him; his only concern was the blood pouring from his hand. I looked around. The effect of the sound of the bullets was as if time had stood still.

'Freeze,' I shouted, waving the gun in a circle to make sure they all knew the threat.

The fight broke up. Bull and Mansion were still having a face-off. The grey-haired man lay on the floor. Stan had his foot on one man's chest; Pieter had his man in an armlock and Red had one man by the throat. Ho had a man in an armlock that he wasn't enjoying physically, let alone his feeling of humiliation. Jesse and the ranch hands had the last man on the table.

'Frisk them,' I called out.

We patted them down — they were all carrying — and put the guns and other weapons on the tables, together with wallets full of cash. We relieved them of the cash and took it to the bartender for the damage done to the bar.

I nodded at Bull. He bent down, dragged the grey-haired man up on to his feet and thrust him down into a chair. I walked across and stood over him.

'Time to talk,' I said. 'What's your name?'

'They call me the Fixer.'

'Not after tonight they won't. Who sent you?

'The man in black, and don't ask me his name 'cos I don't know it.'

'Describe him.'

'Easy. Black suit, black tie, black loafers, mirrored Ray-Bans. Can't see his eyes. Not that you would want to. 'Spect they're black, too. You can tell a lot from the eyes. You wouldn't want to mess with the man in black.'

'Where do you fit in?'

'He picked us up at a diner and offered money for us to stick around for a while and make life difficult for you guys. He pays in cash, which is fine by me.'

'How do you get in touch?'

'He calls us. Tells us where to meet him. I've no way of getting in touch with him, if that's what you want.'

'You got taught a lesson today, Fixer. Now we don't want to see you around here again. Get on your bikes and ride on.'

'What's to stop me coming back with more men?'

'You wouldn't be so stupid. You've seen what we can do — the shot through the palm was just a warning. Next time we'll aim to kill.'

He looked me in the eyes and let out an involuntary shiver.

'You would, too, wouldn't you?' he said.

I nodded and lifted him from the chair. 'Ride on,' I said.

They slunk away, not looking back.

Jesse started clapping and the rest of the ranch hands joined in. They were going to stick around now. Mission accomplished.

* * *

Sheriff Tucker and his deputy were waiting for us outside. I guessed he'd watched the bikers leave before stepping out of the safety of his air-conditioned office. He looked surprised — disappointed, I suspected — to see us in one piece.

'Evening, Sheriff,' I said. 'A fine evening.'

'Well, if it ain't Mr Actually.'

'Then it's someone doing a very good impression.'

He narrowed his eyes and looked at me.

'Are you being funny with me, boy?'

I looked across at Bull — *you're not the only one who gets called 'boy'*.

'Obviously not,' I said. 'Tell me, how's the war against crime going?'

'Seems to be busier since you arrived. The sooner you go, the better for me and the town.'

'We'll go as soon as our job is done.'

'And what would that be?'

'Just as soon as a man can walk into a bar and have a quiet drink or ride his own prairie without being shot at.'

'I'll be watching you boys. Put one foot out of line and I'll have your asses behind bars quicker than you can say jack-rabbit. Now get out.'

I nodded at him and turned to go.

'Jackrabbit,' I said, shaking my head. If it wasn't so dark, I would have seen steam coming out of his ears. All in all, a good night's work.

6

We got up at dawn. Even then there was a heat haze shimmering over the land as the morning dew evaporated. Stan had arranged a rota for keeping watch from the hills and Pieter was to take first shift. He did his press-ups, supervised by Bull, gathered up some sandwiches and water and a pair of binoculars which Stan had picked up in town and, most important of all, the sniper rifle. Red drove him in the jeep and dropped him off. He was due to be relieved by Bull in four hours.

The rest of us gathered round and planned out the day.

'Do you think the bikers will come back?' Stan asked.

'Not if they know what's good for them,' I replied.

'They don't like unfinished business,' said Bull. 'Maybe they're too stubborn to walk away. Or maybe they'll be offered so much money they can't turn it down.'

'My main worry is what the man in black will do next. We put out a warning shot across the bows last night. Will that be enough for them to give up, or will they escalate matters?

Best be prepared.'

'I can't stand hanging around waiting,' said Stan. 'Let's tour the firing positions.'

Each firing position had some form of cover — a tree, large rocks, the side of a building and so on. As we toured, Stan hid a bottle of water and spare ammunition at each position. I still didn't like it. Too many blind spots. But it was the best we could get and we had to hope that the enemy — whoever they turned out to be — didn't get sneaky on us.

When Red returned I told him of my plan for the day. It boiled down to the fact that we had too little information to know who was behind the threats against us. It was time to visit our neighbours and see if they had been experiencing any trouble, or, indeed, if we could find any evidence against them. There was an obvious place to start — the senator.

Around eleven, Red and I set off. We took the horses to give them a workout and to make more of an entrance — also because I had grown kind of fond of Shadow and enjoyed riding him. And, most of all, it meant I didn't have to risk Red's driving — too many ways to die without adding that one.

'You're not going to like what I'm going to say,' said Red as we rode along.

'But that won't stop you saying it.'

'I think you may be coming down too hard on Sheriff Tucker. This is a small town and he doesn't have the resources to take on a bunch of bikers. And if we get this problem sorted out, I've still got to live here. How about making an uneasy peace?'

'Even though he seems as bigoted as the rest?'

'Maybe we can get him to focus on the half of me that is white, rather than the half that is Comanche.'

'If that's what you want, I'll go along with it, but I don't think it will do any good.'

'It's worth a try.'

'I'll go see him this afternoon.'

'Appreciate it,' he said.

We rode on for another thirty minutes and then the ranch came into view. Senator O'Hara's place was like he had modelled it on the Ewing ranch, but had doubled all the measurements. Coming round a sweeping drive you were faced with a long three-storey colonial house with a pillared entrance like the Parthenon. The senator must have been a rider, too, for there was a hitching post and a water trough that looked like it had been carved out of marble. We tied up the horses and walked to the door. There was a black iron handle that you pulled to ring the bell. It was like stepping back a hundred years. Soon, as if someone had been waiting for us, I heard footsteps and the door opened.

'Can I help you, gentlemen?'

The speaker was a short black man, going on sixty, decked out in the full black flunkey outfit, even down to the white gloves.

'Just a neighbourly call,' Red said. 'Is the senator in?'

'I will see, sir,'

Which meant he'd see whether the senator wanted to be bothered by people without an appointment. He waved his arm at two chairs either side of a wide hallway and disappeared somewhere in this maze of a building.

A couple of minutes later and the butler returned. 'The senator will see you on the lawns, sir. Please follow me.'

He led us along the hallway, through a huge sitting room decked out with antique furniture: chairs, tables, sofas, and opulent accessories like they'd been chosen to prop a movie scene: vases, a grandfather clock. We stepped through tall French doors to the garden. There was a wide expanse of manicured lawn surrounded by flower beds full of different coloured roses, jasmine, hibiscus and bougainvillea. The air was heady with their fragrance. It was a fine place to sit and contemplate the world.

The senator was sitting at a large, round,

wooden table. On its top was a pitcher of some sort of drink, a deep bowl of ice and three tumblers. The senator stood up and motioned us to sit down without going through the formalities of shaking our hands. He was wearing a tweed jacket with leather patches on the elbows, beige trousers and brogues, as if he had stepped out of an English country house of the twenties. He was a tall man, but his most striking feature was his slickly combed ginger hair. It looked too good to be true, and if it wasn't, it was the vanity of a middle-aged man.

'What can I do for you gentlemen?'

'Just a social call,' said Red, introducing himself.

O'Hara seemed to press himself back in his chair as if to put as much distance between this half-breed Comanche and himself.

'And you are?' he said to me.

'Johnny Silver,' I replied.

'Not one of the banking dynasty?' he asked.

I nodded modestly and the senator gave me a big smile — one that he probably practised in front of the bathroom mirror each morning. He added ice to two glasses and poured what looked like iced tea complete with sprigs of mint. He passed them across to us. I took an experimental sip. I wasn't going to ask him for the recipe.

'That's good,' I lied. 'You live in some style, Senator. I envy you.'

He gave us another of those smiles.

'Red's been having some trouble,' I said.

He frowned.

'Someone poisoned a stretch of his creek and he's had a couple of run-ins with some bikers.'

'How unfortunate,' he said.

'You could say that,' I said. 'We were wondering if you had experienced anything similar.'

'Now you come to mention it, I think there was something about some steers dying under suspicious circumstances; well, unexplained at least. You'd have to talk to my foreman for the details.' He raised a hand in the air and clicked his fingers. 'Jackson,' he called.

The butler appeared out of nowhere and walked across to the table.

'Jackson. Ask Slim to come here at once.'

The butler nodded and walked slowly back into the house. If I had been him, I would have walked more quickly. It must have been like being in a sauna in that monkey suit with gloves and all. Maybe you got used to the heat. That seemed to be what everybody said, but I still didn't believe it.

The senator moved his chair slightly so that he was facing me and Red was out of his immediate vision.

'First trip to the States?' he said.

I nodded and wondered where this was going.

'Mighty fine country,' O'Hara said. 'A man can make his dreams come true here.'

Did that include Jackson, or did he not count? Did it include Red, for that matter?

A man came out of the house. He was tall and wore a hat, sand-coloured chinos, an open-neck shirt matching the trousers and cowboy boots with Cuban heels. He approached the table, doffed his hat to O'Hara. He had hard features — nose, chin, cheekbones — like he had been chiselled out of a block of granite.

'Slim,' the senator said. 'Meet Mr Silver and . . . ?'

'Red. Just Red will do.'

'Slim,' O'Hara said. 'Mr Silver would like to know if we have been experiencing any trouble recently?'

'Anything out of the normal,' I added.

Slim pondered the question. He ran his fingers through his blond hair and nodded as if it was all coming back to him.

'While back,' he said, 'someone had put tacks on the ground by the stable — caused a couple of horses to go lame. One of the guard dogs got poisoned. Then we had some steers rustled — that won't happen again, I've tightened up security since then.'

'What did the sheriff say? Presumably you reported the rustling episode, at least?'

'Tucker said he'd like to help, but he didn't have the men to keep watch on the place and we should organize something ourselves. I now have one man who just works nights and keeps a look-out over the land. It's an inconvenience, that's all.'

'Thanks, Slim,' said O'Hara.

Slim doffed his hat again and headed back to the house.

'Any ideas who might be behind those incidents?' I asked. 'Got any enemies?'

'Could be some ex-employee with a grudge. Political opponent, maybe. But it's all a little trivial for that.' He stood up, signalling the audience was over. 'Good to see you,' he said.

'Another white man who speaks with forked tongue,' whispered Red as we walked back to the house.

'Hell, he's a politician. What did you expect?'

* * *

I drove into town, stopped off at a liquor store and bought a bottle of bourbon, then stepped into the sheriffs office. There was no deputy there today, just Tucker, seated at his desk reading through a manila file of papers. He looked over the top of the papers and looked down again.

'Red would say, 'Smoke pipe of peace', but I'm hoping bourbon will do just as well.'

I took the bottle of bourbon out of the brown paper bag and put it on his desk.

He considered me for a moment, shook his head as if to get to grips with such an unexpected move, then got up and went over to a tall grey filing cabinet. He took out two tumblers, placed them on the desk and poured a big measure into each of them. He slid one across to me, then leaned back in his chair and put his hands behind his head.

I raised my glass and took a sip.

'You got some nerve,' he said.

'Sometimes I just can't resist the temptation to be a wise guy.'

'That I've noticed.'

He took a swig of his bourbon and looked at me with half-closed eyes.

'You know,' he said, 'this used to be a peaceable town. Since Red arrived it's been nothing but trouble.'

'You can't blame the trouble on Red. Take last night. A bunch of bikers arrive looking to cause a fight, or at least to frighten us off coming to town again.'

'Yeah, yeah. But Red is the catalyst.

Trouble has even spread to the senator — you heard about the rustling and stuff? I'm left wondering where it will go next.'

He topped up our glasses and took an appreciative sip.

'Time's gone by when me and the deputy could pretty much run the town without much intervention — the odd Saturday night drunk or kids racing each other in cars, but how am I supposed to handle a bunch of bikers who are armed to the teeth? What's my deputy's wife gonna say if he gets himself killed? I kinda think it's not our fight.'

'So what's Red supposed to do? Sell up and move away? Where's the justice in that?'

'It would solve my problems.'

I gave him a long, hard look.

'OK,' he said. He raised his hands, palms facing me. 'I could see if I can get some help from the State police, but they won't be able to stick around for long. They won't be prepared to play a waiting game.'

'What about if we form an agreement? You let us get on with protecting Red, his men and his property, and we'll keep you out of the picture. In effect, we'll do your job for you.'

'Are you asking me to sanction a posse of vigilantes?'

'I like to think of it more as turning a blind

eye. You haven't got the resources, so you said, to protect the town from outside forces. We're used to that kind of work, We're professionals — we can handle ourselves. When we have finally sorted out this problem, we'll bring you in to make the arrests and take the glory.'

'That sounds like bribery. You're digging yourself a hole.'

'I'm trying to find a way that we can both coexist — not treading on each other's toes, so to speak.'

'I'll tell you what I'll do. What's happening in this town ain't good for business — we get a lot of tourists here and they expect to be able to walk the streets without fear. If you can keep your quarrel private — away from town — I'll turn that blind eye. But if there's any more shooting like last night in a bar or maybe in a store or on the streets, I'll come down heavy on anyone I can get — and that includes you. Do what you have to do and then get out of my town. Agreed?'

I nodded: it was the best deal I was going to get. We touched glasses and I drained mine.

'Thanks, Sheriff,' I said, getting up.

'You disappoint me,' he said.

'Why?'

'I had you down for some fancy stuff like

modus vivendi, actually.'

I smiled and made my exit.

Across the street I could see Jerome and his dog sitting on the porch. I walked over and scratched the dog's head.

'Heard you had some trouble last night,' he said.

'Nothing we couldn't handle,' I said.

'They'll be back,' he said.

I raised an eyebrow.

'I heard them talking as they rode off. They're gonna raise an army and hit you again.'

'I was rather hoping they would have seen sense.'

'What would you do in the same place?'

'Hard to lose face,' I said. 'Especially when you're part of a group where image is all important. I'd like to think that I'd ride on.'

'But?'

'But I'd probably come back better prepared.'

'That's what I thought,' he said, nodding his head wisely.

The dog nuzzled up against me and I scratched his head some more.

'See much of Jackson?' I asked, changing the subject to something less threatening.

'We black guys got to support each other in a town like this. We get together every Sunday — it's his night off — play chequers, have some whiskey. What do you want to know?'

'There's a lot about the senator I don't trust. Would be good to have his view.'

'I'll do what I can,' he said. 'Come see me Monday. And bring some peanuts for the dog — he may be old, but he's got a good memory.'

'And not just the dog,' I said.

* * *

The guys were thrilled at the prospect of another run in with the bikers. There was silence around the dining table after I had broken the news.

'Defences,' Stan said. 'We need to create some defences that will thin their numbers before they reach us.' He stood up and looked closely at the map. 'There's only one road in and out. We can force them off that and make them go across country where their bikes will be a hindrance. Then we need to create some barriers — ditches, pits, whatever.'

'How many of the ranch hands can you spare, Red?' I asked.

'Three, maybe four, but that's cutting my workforce to the bone. Old man Blenkenstein's got a digger — been trying to dig for another source of water. I'm sure he won't object to lending it to us.'

'We'll go to see him tomorrow,' I said to Red. 'Stan, make a list of what we need, then go into town first thing in the morning and pick up everything. Then it's all hands to the pumps.'

Stan studied the map again. 'We can do this,' he said. 'We'll give those bikers a surprise they won't forget for a long while. This time they'll learn that it doesn't pay to mess with us.' There was the sound of excitement in his normally morose voice. He stabbed at various points on the map. 'Yeah, we can do this.'

The mood lightened. We had faith in Stan to make it work.

It was going to be one hell of a fight.

7

Bull, Red and I drove to the Alamo Retreat. It was a fine evening, the heat of the day had dissipated and there was a small breeze blowing off the mountains. The moon was starting to rise and cast a silver shadow over the land. It was almost romantic, and might work in our favour, or Pieter's as he had a special role. On either side of the tarmac track that led to the retreat there was lush pasture, but no animals were taking advantage of it. Around a bend a large farmhouse came into view. It was typical for the area, not as lavish as Senator O'Hara's spread but a similar size to Red's and it appeared to be well maintained. There were a few dozen people making their way from the fields to the farmhouse, mostly women dressed in white and carrying wicker baskets, the few men looking like they'd been turning over the soil or doing something else manual that involved a lot of dirt. They were singing. It seemed like an old-fashioned plantation in the Deep South where the slaves would harmonize to make the work seem easier and time go more quickly.

Fey and the two girls were waiting at the door of the farmhouse to greet us. Fey was dressed in a long white shift dress that seemed to flow for ever and finished just above her peasant-style rope-soled espadrilles. The two girls were also wearing long dresses, Cameron's a light brown and Lucy's a shade of blue that matched her eyes.

'So glad you could come,' said Fey excitedly. 'Please come inside.'

The door opened on a large square room with Native American rugs on the floors and multicoloured blankets on the walls. If the room had been conical, you might have mistaken it for a giant tepee. A series of long refectory tables in oak, bleached by time and scrubbing to a dull white, had been pushed together. On either side of the tables were benches. There were vases of flowers placed at various points on the tables. All very homely.

At the far end of the room was a large wingback chair. From the chair arose a tall, slim man in a thigh-length kaftan over loose-fitting trousers. He had long blond hair, was tanned and looked healthy. He held his hands out in a gesture of embrace and walked toward us.

'I am Rafael,' he said. 'Welcome to our house.'

His voice was quiet and serene, the kind that could make you drift off into a hypnotic sleep if you listened for too long.

I made the introductions and he beckoned us to sit on the benches along the tables. He took the head, with myself at his right side, rapidly joined by Lucy, who held my hand: Red sat opposite me with Cameron holding his arm; Fey sat next to Bull; they looked an odd pair because of their contrasting physiques and colouring. Others started coming in — maybe twenty or so, their faces glowing from a fresh wash and brush up — and joined us.

Bowls of food were brought in, steam rising from them. I tried to guess what they were as they were laid upon the table: some sort of brown rice; beansprouts; a tomato-coloured dish with green herbs sprinkled on top, which I was hoping was exactly that; bright yellow sweetcorn. There were baskets piled high with brown bread. Meagre fare. It wasn't looking too good for us carnivores.

By each place-setting there was an earthenware goblet. Two women, also dressed in white, placed jugs of apple juice and iced water on the table. No chance of a beer, I guessed.

Everyone looked down and Rafael said a short prayer. Following this, the bowls of food circulated and we all helped themselves. Red, Bull and I took cautiously small portions. Wise move — it was bland, far too healthy and totally unsatisfying. Still, you can't have steak and chips every day; there's always tomorrow.

'We have to thank you,' Rafael said to me, 'for what you did for Lucy. If you hadn't been able to rescue her when the horse bolted I don't know what would have happened to her.'

'All part of the service,' I said.

'No, you're too modest. Most men would simply have sat there and watched. We owe you a great debt.'

'When someone's shooting at you,' Bull said, 'the last thing you want to do is sit there like a fish in a barrel.'

'And why should anyone want to shoot at you?' Rafael asked.

'That's what we're trying to find out,' I said. 'What about you? Anything suspicious happened to you? Any threats? It's still possible that the person who fired the shot was aiming at Fey, or Cameron or Lucy.'

'Why should anyone want to cause trouble for us? We don't represent any sort of threat to anyone.'

'Where there are bigots involved,' I said, 'some people don't need an excuse. It could be that what you do here might be a threat to their Stone-Age values. From what I've seen of this town, people aren't that friendly towards strangers.'

'Maybe they just need some time to get adjusted to Red being around,' Rafael said. 'Being a half-breed isn't an easy life. Ask Cameron.'

'Has someone been threatening you?' Red asked, grasping her hand.

'No, not as such,' she said, her dark eyes fixed on him. 'When I first came here and went into town the people used to step aside from me, like I had some kind of disease. They don't do it so much now.' She squeezed his arm tenderly. 'Give them time.'

'Time seems to be running out,' I said. 'The situation gets worse rather than better.'

'You could pray,' Rafael said, as if it were the solution to everything. I wished I had his faith, whatever that was.

There was an awkward silence.

'Pass the apple juice, please,' Cameron said, breaking the spell. 'We press it ourselves from the apples in our orchard. Everything you see on the table is the fruit of our labours.'

I passed the pitcher across the table, poured juice in her goblet and looked at Rafael.

'Tell me about yourself,' I said, 'and what you do here.'

'The Retreat is an autonomous group of individuals that is self-sufficient in the main and asks no more than to be left in peace.'

'Left in peace to do what?' I asked.

'To provide sanctuary for those who need it, for whatever reason. Take Cameron, for instance. She is half Cheyenne, half Scots and was left with nowhere to go and no one to care for her when she ran away from home. She came here when she was just twelve years old and we have been her family ever since, and will always be so.'

'You said sanctuary for whatever reason. Does that include those who break the law?'

'We form our own judgements on transgressors of the law. Sometimes you have to break the law to do the right thing.'

'There we agree with you. But we're in the minority.'

'One day society will catch up to our views.'

'Don't hold your breath,' I said.

He smiled, a little condescendingly I thought.

'What do you do for money?' I asked. 'There must be some things you need beyond the fruits of your self-sufficiency.'

'When I was twenty-one I came into an

inheritance from my grandfather. That was just enough to buy the land here and get us started. We eat what we grow and raise extra money by selling our surplus crops and by making various craft items such as baskets, jewellery, embroidery and so on.'

'And how do you govern yourselves?'

'We are a democratic commune.'

'But Rafael is wise,' Fey said. 'We give ourselves up to him as leader. If we want a vote, it will be given, but there is rarely any need. We know that Rafael has our best interests at heart.'

Therefore, if I read her right, Rafael called the shots. Nothing wrong with benevolent dictators, until they lose their benevolence and then they're just dictators.

'So you haven't had any trouble?' I said.

Rafael nodded. Lucky him.

'How do you get on with your neighbours?' I asked.

'The Blenkensteins keep pretty much to themselves. We don't force ourselves on people, don't try to convert them. We're wise enough to know that our life doesn't suit everybody.'

'And how about the senator?' Bull asked. 'I very much doubt he would share your tolerance.'

'O'Hara leaves us alone. Grudgingly, I

suspect, but he and my father go way back. My father runs a big company that donates money to the senator's political fund. O'Hara wants to stand for president one day.'

'God preserve us,' Red said somewhat irreverently, but Rafael took it with a grin. Red shook his head. 'Could set this country back fifty years. Only now we don't have a Martin Luther King.'

'Where there is injustice,' Rafael said, 'someone will always come forward to stand against it.'

'I wish I had your confidence, or your optimism,' I said.

Bull looked at his watch. I knew what he was thinking. Sentry duty starting soon.

'Thanks for the meal,' I said, 'and the neighbourly hospitality.' To Fey I said, 'Bring the girls over some time and we'll go riding together. Give it a while though, so that things can settle down.'

'Yes, please, Fey,' Lucy said. 'Promise.'

'I promise,' she said.

We rose from the table, Lucy still clutching my hand and Cameron clinging to her new half-breed friend, Red. Kindred spirits. I hoped that Rafael's luck would hold and they didn't get victimized, too. We would have to protect them and that would stretch our limited resources thinner. Not a good strategy.

We were pensive for a while on the way back, then I broke the silence.

'I hope they don't get drawn into your problems, Red,' I said. 'They'll just roll over so as to avoid any conflict. Won't stand a chance.'

'Could be picking us off one by one,' Bull said. 'If Red gives in and moves out, they'll know it does no good to resist.'

'The same thought occurred to me,' I said. 'In a town as bigoted as this, someone like Rafael with all his peace and love ideas could get under someone's skin. What you don't understand poses a threat. It will be the slippery-slope theory — let Rafael and his people gain a foothold here and who knows what will happen next.'

'Best not to think of it,' Red said.

'Best to think of it and form a plan,' I said. 'What I don't understand is why Cameron and Lucy are there. They're just kids, can't make the kind of life-changing decisions that adults can. Haven't got the experience to make a rational choice.'

'According to Fey, who told me quietly over what they call a meal, they've both got histories,' Bull said. 'Sad ones. Fey came across Lucy at the airport. She was begging. Looked like she hadn't eaten for days, or slept for that matter. Turned out her dad had died of cancer and she was left with the wicked stepmother. Treated like a slave. Got beaten if she didn't do as she was told — maybe even beaten when she did. At the time in life when she needed a father figure or a male role model, she had no one to turn to. One day she couldn't take it any longer. Packed her bags and hitched to the airport — thought she might get some money from the travellers and be able to sleep in the departures lounge. If the Retreat hadn't found her, God knows what would have become of her — she was easy prey. Probably would have finished up on the streets.'

Not a nice thought. Sounded like the only route for her would have been downhill, and all the way, too.

'And Cameron?' Red asked.

'Similar sort of story, except this time her father, the Cheyenne side of her make-up, was a drunk. Used to slap her around. One day he tried to get into bed with her. She beat him off and told her mother. Mother wasn't able to stand on her own two feet and needed a man — any man, even a bad one would do. Said she didn't believe Cameron — that she was just trying to get attention. Cameron had no option but to run away or face a life of abuse. She was heading for Mexico, for some strange reason — sounded glamorous, I suspect. She hitched a ride and the driver was a local man and told her about the Retreat. He offered to take her there. Cameron thought she had nothing to lose. She liked what she saw — free and easy lifestyle — and stayed. Another one missing a father figure and male role model. It's going to be tricky for us — especially Red and Johnny — to act properly, but not to get too involved. They're likely to hang on to whichever of us, in their eyes, fills in that missing element, fills the void that they both have.'

'What about Fey?' asked Red.

'Been a long time since I saw someone as beautiful as her,' Bull said.

'Don't let Anna know you said that,' I warned. 'I'd have to defend her and it's not good to have fighting in the ranks.'

I nodded. 'And what's Fey's story?'

'She's just a free spirit. Pretty much a flashback to the sixties — love and peace, goodwill to all men and all that jazz.'

'No harm in that,' Red said. 'World would be a better place if more people felt that way.'

'She's an innocent,' Bull said. 'Can't see the evil around or the bad side of people. In her way she's as vulnerable as Lucy and Cameron. She's loaded, too. Lots of people would like to take advantage of that.'

'Where's her money come from?' I asked.

'Inheritance,' Pieter said. 'Grandmother was a cute businesswoman with good advisors. Saw the dotcom boom, made some shrewd investments, cashed in at the right time. Heart attack got her. Fey came into the money when she was eighteen. Got involved with a bunch of musicians, took off from restrictive parents, did the festival circuit, met Rafael at one of them — good recruiting opportunity for the Retreat — and liked his ideas.'

'How much has she given to Rafael?'

'Nothing. He doesn't need it. If he does, then Fey will bankroll Rafael and the community. But they don't need it. You've seen the simple way they live. Self-sufficient — don't want for anything.'

'Anything else we should know?' I said.

'No, that just about covers it.'

'OK,' I said. 'I'll phone Stan.'

'Why's that?'

'To see if he can organize some sandwiches. I'm starving.'

Bull and Red nodded their agreement.

'I could even eat one of his beloved dill pickles,' Bull said.

'Then all's well that ends well,' I said.

'Let's hope,' said Red. 'Let's hope.'

* * *

Bull had woken me for my shift at two o'clock. I made a mug of strong coffee and took it out to the porch. I placed the Uzi on the floor on my right side, the Browning in my lap and cradled the mug between both hands. I looked slowly around and saw nothing moving. If anyone came, I was ready for him.

The bunkhouse door opened and out came Jesse.

'Couldn't sleep,' he said. 'Mind if I join you?'

I gestured to the chair on my left.

'Do you mind if I talk?' he said.

He was nervous. Knew that there was a fight brewing and wondered how he would react. That's what everyone thinks. You train and practise, over and over again, but it's only when the battle starts that you find out what you're going to do.

'Go ahead,' I said. 'It'll help pass the time.'

'Where do you live?' he asked.

'A little island paradise in the Caribbean called St Jude. Got a wife and soon I'll have a child, too. Run a bar there. Doesn't get much better than that. What about you?'

'No wife, no kids. Just kind of drifted around from place to place. Never put any roots down. That's fine when you're young,' he shook his head, 'but gets kinda lonely at my age.'

'What are your plans?'

'Same as most ranch hands. Put a little stash together and buy a farm of my own. Nothing fancy, but big enough to keep a few pigs and chickens, grow some corn. Get the fruits of my labour rather than working for someone else. Don't get me wrong, I like working here. Red's a good boss. Trusts you to do your job, not on your back all the time like some bosses. But it's not the same as having your own place.'

I nodded. Guessed it was a familiar story. Ranch hands, I suspected, couldn't help blow their wages on gambling, booze or nights at the local whorehouse. Always falling short of that bankroll.

'I guess what I'm saying,' Jesse said, 'is that I'd like to help. Got nothing to lose. Would make me feel like I done something worthwhile with my life. It ain't right what someone's doing to Red.'

'Can you shoot?' I asked.

'Never tried, but it don't look that difficult.'

'You're right,' I said. 'Shooting's easy; it's hitting the target that's difficult. Most of the time you only get one shot and you have to make that count or you're dead.'

'You could teach me,' he said.

'We'll start in the morning,' I said. 'Now get some sleep. You never know what tomorrow will bring.'

8

We sat around the table drinking coffee and staring at Stan's pictograms on the map he had drawn.

'We have to assume,' Stan said, 'that they will approach by the main track from the road. There's no reason why they should do anything else, and if they are true bikers they won't want to damage their tyres or suspension by going cross-country. That's what we will be doing.'

'OK,' I said, 'so the track will be our first line of defence?'

'We construct barriers along the side of the track,' Stan said, pointing to two lines on the map, 'so that they act as a funnel. Then we dig a big pit, cover it with tarpaulin and disguise it with earth so that it blends in.'

'I can see that the first few lines of bikes will drop into the pit,' I said, 'but the rest will soon wise up. What's your plans for them?'

'Stingers,' Sam said. 'We put rolls of barbed wire across the track after the pit. Their tyres will puncture and then they'll be on foot — those who haven't given up by then, that is. We should be able to cut down their numbers — they are reckoning to outnumber us ten to one and have an easy time. Each time they meet a trap they will get demoralized.'

'And a demoralized army is a beaten army,' Bull said. 'I'm liking this.'

'It means that we will have to take a detour when we leave or enter the ranch,' Stan said, 'but our jeeps and trucks can handle that easily. Anyone got any other ideas?'

'I'd like to have an added exit through the Alamo's land,' I said. 'Nothing major: just replace one length of fence with a simple bar-and-pole fence. Something we can easily dismantle and ride or drive through.'

'Or enable them to get here if they face any problems,' Red said. 'So far they haven't had any trouble, but I'd feel happier if they had somewhere to run. We don't have the manpower to guard their land, too.'

'What about adding some trip wires?' Pieter said. 'Thin wire at waist level for the bikers. That should whittle them down further.'

Stan nodded. 'Here would be the best place,' he said, stabbing at the map. 'Maybe fifty yards back from the stingers so that they get the feeling that they have got over the obstacles and have a clear run from there.'

'Oil might work, too,' Red said. 'More

tarpaulin, this time covered with oil. After that, place something hard for them to skid into.'

'Looks like we've got a plan,' Bull said. 'When we start digging the pit and making all the other traps, we'll need a guard on the road to stop anyone sneaking a look at what we're doing. Can you add that to your rota, Stan, of what our duties are at various times of the day?'

'It means we are another person committed,' he replied. 'It will mean longer shifts on the foothills of the mountain and everywhere else we stand guard. We are starting to stretch ourselves a bit thin.'

'We can draft in Jesse,' I said. 'He's keen to help.'

'Okay,' Stan said. 'I'll work it out later. The first priority is getting all the gear that we need.'

'Do a list. I promised Jesse some shooting practice — he could go into town after we finish that. Pick himself up a gun while he's there. I'm not suggesting he should get involved in the heat of the battle, but just for his own protection. We'll use him as one of the lookouts. Once he's spotted any action he gets back here to the ranch house and we take over.' I took one last look at the map and fixed the plan in my mind. 'OK, guys, let's have action. I'll spend an hour with Jesse and then we'll go to see the Blenkensteins, Red.'

Pieter picked up the sniper rifle and a bottle of water and headed off to the foothills, with Bull driving him there. Stan started to make his list. As I was about to walk out of the room Bull held up his hand to stop me.

'Johnny,' he said. 'Is this going to work?'

'I can't think of anything better,' I answered.

'Somehow I hoped that would sound more reassuring,' he said.

'Me too,' I replied.

* * *

Jesse and I were lying prone on the grass behind a large rock that was the most forward of our firing positions. He had my gun in his right hand and had extended it as if to shoot. We'd set up a bale of hay about fifty yards away and marked it in blue paint with a silhouette of a standing man.

'Can I start shooting?' he asked enthusiastically.

'Not yet. Let's start with some basics. There are three things you need to remember about handling a gun. The first is to squeeze the trigger. If you just pull it or yank at it, then the gun jerks and you will miss the target.'

Jesse nodded, and I continued: 'The second thing is that your hand is liable to shake, especially if you are a beginner, so you need to find something to rest the gun on. This rock will do for our purposes.'

He nodded again. Must have all sounded easy at this stage.

'What's the third thing?' he asked.

'The third thing is that the first two points should be irrelevant. Your job is simply to fire one shot and get the hell out of here. The sound of the shot will alert us and we'll take up our pre-rehearsed firing positions. You just concentrate on getting back to the ranch house as quickly as your legs will carry you. Oh, and run zigzag fashion so you're less of a target.'

'I think I can handle that,' he said. 'Now can I start shooting?'

'Not yet. You need to release the safety catch.' I showed him where it was and he looked at me eagerly. 'Now you can start shooting.'

He rested the barrel of the gun on top of the rock and squeezed the trigger as commanded. The bale of hay just sat there.

'This is trickier than it looks,' he said.

'The cowboy films make it look too easy. Think of the gun as an extension of your right arm. Run your middle finger along the barrel if that helps.'

He took up a new stance. Fired again. Clipped the top right hand corner of the bale.

'You've just shot your assailant in the left shoulder. Aim slightly down and to your left.'

'That will take it too low. Shouldn't I be aiming at his head?'

'I don't want anyone killed unnecessarily. Shoot him in the stomach and he will go down and the fight will go out of him. You can forget about him then. Shoot him in the heart and you'll never be able to forget about it. It'll haunt you all your days. You'll never be the same man again. Plus, if you kill him, it's going to take a lot of good answers to get us off a murder charge. Sheriff Tucker would love that.'

'You've killed, haven't you, Johnny?'

'Only when there was no other option. If it's a choice of him or me, then you have to resort to killing him. But I've never enjoyed it like some people. Some get a kick from it — it's the ultimate power, that of life or death. They are the ones you have to watch out for, for they will kill without any warning signs and they don't have any scruples, like shooting a man in the back. In my book, you have to justify killing or you can't live with yourself. With this bunch of bikers I intend to give them every opportunity to turn round and ride on. If they want a fight, we'll be ready and that means ready to kill. I always hope it won't come to that.'

'How do you tell which ones will kill without hesitation from the ones that don't pose that much of a threat?'

'You look at their eyes, inside their eyes. That's where you see it.'

'And you and the others have that look, haven't you. I've seen it. Like that night in town. None of you would pull back. It makes me shiver.'

'If you see that look in anyone's eyes, get out,' I said. 'Now you can shoot again. Imagine that bale of hay is your enemy. The one with the look. You can't get away, so it's time for you to shoot. Go ahead.'

He lined up the gun again and squeezed the trigger twice. Both shots hit as he intended: the bale shifted back from the impact of the two bullets. He smiled at me, pleased with himself.

'And again,' I said. 'Three shots this time. Just in case it's beginner's luck.'

He fired off three rounds which all hit the target in the middle. He gave a bigger smile this time and extended his hand to shake mine.

'Well done,' I said. 'Now just pray you don't have to use your new-found skill.'

* * *

The sun was high by the time Red and I set off for the Blenkensteins. The approach to their farm was along a rutted dirt track. There was a post box at the start of the track. No wonder. What postman would want to drive up that track every day. The four-wheel-drive jeep took it in its stride, but it was a bumpy ride and would have done some damage to the suspension of a lesser vehicle.

To our left, along the border with the Alamo Retreat, we could see people working in the fields, picking corncobs. Ahead, the fields were populated with a few cows, a pigsty big enough for maybe six sows and their offspring, and some kind of crop — wheat, it looked like to my ignorant eyes — that needed harvesting. The ranch house was little bigger than a cabin and needed a coat of paint. In the background we could see the digger that we hoped to borrow. The digger, which looked like it had hardly been used, seemed out of place among the tumbledown nature of the farm.

As we pulled up, the Blenkensteins came out to meet us. The woman was wearing a long black dress and was wiping her hands on a white apron. She had grey hair done up in a bun and was somewhere in her sixties, and, appropriately, wearing a pair of round granny-glasses. The man was probably a few years older, with thinning grey hair. He wore a pair of black trousers, a grey shirt that once might have been white, and red braces. He walked stiffly as if he had a bad back or arthritis in his lower body. Running a place like this must have added years to their lives: it was too big for an old couple. If it was me, I would have sold up and bought a little retirement home to while away my days.

'Good to see you, Red,' Mr Blenkenstein said. 'And you, too, mister.'

He put an arm around Red and led him inside the cabin.

He spoke with an accent that sounded, from the lisp that accompanied the words, like Dutch. I wondered how long they had owned the place and whether the accent had softened with the years or if he had stubbornly hung on to it as a reminder of the past.

Inside, there was a iron stove with a coffee pot on top, an immaculate kitchen with the smell of baking pastry, and a combined dining and living area. The dining table probably seated about eight and the living quarters had two large sofas and a rocking chair with a newspaper on the seat. For two people it was adequate; that was about all that one could say about it.

'Coffee?' Mrs Blenkenstein said, motioning us towards the dining table.

We nodded our heads and she poured a thick black liquid into two small cups. Which was good — you didn't want a large mug of this stuff. It had been sat stewing on that stove for far too long and now tasted bitter and burnt.

'A piece of pie?' she asked, her lined face breaking into a smile. 'Growing boys like you need building up.'

Neither of us had the nerve to say no. We wanted that digger and couldn't afford to get on the wrong side of them.

She cut two large slices of an apple pie that actually looked and smelt pretty good. I took an experimental bite. It was like a cross between a pie and a strudel, spiced with cloves and dotted with raisins.

'This is good, ma'am,' I said. 'I'm Johnny, an old friend of Red. Good to get to meet you.'

'And to make your acquaintance,' Mrs Blenkenstein said.

'To what do we owe the honour of your visit?' Mr Blenkenstein asked. 'Not that it isn't always good to see you, Red.'

'We're doing some work at the ranch,' Red said, glossing over any details that might be useful to an enemy if they ever found out, 'and were hoping to borrow your digger — just a couple days would do fine, if it wouldn't be an inconvenience.'

There was a slight hesitation during which he was no doubt evaluating whether we could be trusted with his pristine digger and what we would think if he refused.

'Where are you going to be digging?' he asked. 'The ground gets harder as you near the mountains. Don't want you wasting your time.'

'Just some work in front of the ranch,' Red said. 'Shouldn't take more than a day or so.'

Mr Blenkenstein thought about this for a second or two, then nodded his head.

'I'll bring it over later,' he said. 'Seeing as how I'm used to driving the thing — sometimes it seems to have a mind of its own.'

'How's the well going?' Red asked.

'It's a slow business. Like I said, the ground's hard — full of rock from the mountains once you get through the top layer; even the digger struggles to break it. I get the feeling it's either that rock or me, and that the damned rock is winning.'

I couldn't help smiling. I got the feeling that the damned rock didn't stand a chance.

'How long have you lived here?' I said.

'We go back thirty years, this place and us.

Thirty years of scratching a living.'

'It's hard work being a farmer,' I said, noticing his calloused hands for the first time. 'I'm not sure I could do it. Not got the patience.'

'Farming teaches you that you don't get nothing without hard work,' he said. 'Except for Red, that is. He's a lucky son of a gun.'

'Almost my words exactly,' I said.

'There was a time,' he said with eyes that grew dark, 'when it weren't so hard. When we had Ray, our son, doing all the heavy work. But when he died it was all up to me and Ma. Can't afford no help, so it's up to the two of us.'

Ma Blenkenstein nodded and looked away.

'I'm sorry,' Red said. 'I could have offered you some help if I had known.'

'I hear you need all the hands you've got — and then some.'

'What else do you hear?' I asked.

'That someone's going to run you out of town, one way or another.'

'That someone doesn't know me, or my friends,' Red said.

'Ray thought he was immortal, too. Then the big C got him. We ain't got no church around here for our faith — we're Evangelicals, or Lutherans as you folks insist on calling us — so we buried him out back six foot under. Some day we'll join him. One way or another, we're not going to leave this place.'

Ma Blenkenstein got up and went across to the window over the kitchen sink. She stared out as if something fascinating was happening outside. She took a handkerchief out of her apron pocket and blew her nose loudly.

'I'm sorry,' I said. 'It must be hard to bury your own son. When did this happen?'

'He got sick about a year ago and then gradually got worse and worse. After six months he was bedridden and then he lingered for a while. That was the hardest part, seeing him get thinner and weaker each day till he was just a shadow of himself. He died a month ago. It was a blessing. Since then me and Ma have been picking up the pieces as best we can.'

I felt for the both of them — outliving your children is something no parent wants to do. I wished I'd kept my big mouth shut and hadn't asked questions that made them rake over the past. I looked at Red and he read my mind.

'You call on us whenever you need help,' he said, 'harvest time or whatever. It won't matter if we've got problems. We'll be there for you. That's what neighbours are for.'

'Well, thanks, Red,' Pa Blenkenstein said.

He had a tear in his eye and quickly brushed it away with the frayed cuff of his sleeve. 'Now, about this digger. I'll bring it over this evening and show you how it works. Keep it as long as you like — my well can wait.'

We shook hands. There was nothing left to say.

9

We had finished for the day and were seated around the table awaiting Jesse with his third load of materials and Pa Blenkenstein with his digger. There was a bucket of ice stocked with cans of beer on the porch ready for us to watch the sun go down. We were feeling like we were progressing pretty well with our plan. Tomorrow would be the day that would tell us how long our traps would take to assemble.

A silver Mercedes came along the drive and parked at the side of the bunkhouse. I gestured to the others and we took our places on the porch. I gestured Red to take up the position furthest on the right. We were armed and ready for anything that might ensue.

A man, in his thirties I guessed from the athletic way he walked, got out of the car. He was wearing Ray-Ban Aviators with mirror lenses, a lightweight black suit, white shirt with a button-down collar, black tie and black loafers. Our presence didn't seem to intimidate him. I noticed his jacket was unbuttoned and bulged slightly under his left arm. He was packing. Still, he must have had guts to face odds of five to one.

'Who's the boss man?' he said, looking along the line of us.

'I guess that would be me,' I said. 'You got a name?'

'Name's not important,' he said. 'Message is.'

I kind of liked his style. I wondered what we could do to throw him off balance.

'And the message is?' I said.

'There are people who think you don't belong here. What will it take to buy you out?'

'Which people?' I said.

'I'm not at liberty to disclose that,' he said.

'Not even if I give you a Chinese burn?' I said.

His mouth started to turn up into a smile, but he fought it.

'I'm authorized to make you an offer of two million dollars,' he said.

'Hardly generous,' I said. 'What's the place worth to you, Red?'

'This place is my home. Hard to put a value on your home. A lot more than two million, though.'

'Think about it,' he said. 'The place only has value as long as you can farm it. Hard to do with no labour. Things could get hot around here.'

'Things are always hot around here,' I said.

'This offer will only be made once. After

that the price goes down. Think about it.'

'Not much to think about,' I said

'Pass me a beer,' he said.

I took a beer from the bucket and threw the can towards him. He caught it deftly and, in one movement, tossed the can in the air. He pulled out his gun and put three bullets in the can before it hit the ground. He looked me in the eye. Better that, his look said.

'See that tree,' I said, pointing to an apple tree around thirty yards away. It had seen better days, several of the branches being dead and bare.

He looked at the tree and then back at me. He nodded.

I took out the Browning from the back of my waistband. Took aim and clipped two inches off the end of a branch.

He made like he wasn't impressed. After all, I could have been aiming anywhere on the tree.

'Bull,' I said.

Bull drew his gun and fired. Clipped an inch off the end of the same branch.

'Stan,' I said. 'You next.'

Stan repeated the process. Then Pieter. Finally, it was Red's turn. He reached down by his side and drew the shotgun. Boom! The left-hand side of the apple tree turned to shreds.

'I think you've got your answer,' I said.
'I'll be back,' he said.
'Let us know and we'll bake you a cake.'

* * *

The digger arrived just before the sun went down. There was enough light to cast an eye over it and mark out the key controls. It didn't seem too difficult provided you had good coordination. Clutch, accelerator, forward and reverse gears, a lever to raise and lower the bucket, one to tip and one to move sideways left and right. I was itching to use it and hoped it would make fast work of digging our pit. We could only hope, since we couldn't know how much time we had. I looked up and saw a flashing blue light in the distance: it seemed to be heading our way.

The sheriff pulled up in front of the house and got out of his car, its light still flashing.

'We found Jesse,' he said.

'I didn't know he was lost,' I said.

'Now's not the time to be pedantic,' Tucker said. 'He's in a bad way. Someone beat him up pretty good. We're waiting for an ambulance to take him to hospital. You better follow me into town.'

I asked Stan and Pieter to stay behind on guard and Bull and I jumped into the back of the four-wheel-drive and let Red drive — time was of the essence and Red would get us there faster than the sheriff, given an overtaking opportunity.

A little way outside the town we saw the truck. It had pulled up half on the road and half on the scrub verge. The deputy was bending down beside it. Jesse was on the floor, covered with a coat. Red slewed the vehicle to a halt; the three of us jumped out and joined the deputy.

Jesse's face was a mess. The sheriff was right — someone had done a thorough job on him. Both eyes were reduced to slits and there was blood trickling from his mouth and from a gash on his head. I lifted the coat gently and cast an eye over his body. His arm was lying in an impossible position, a fragment of bone sticking out. There was blood soaking through his shirt: I guessed broken ribs — if he was lucky. I prayed there was no internal bleeding. He looked up at me.

'Who did this?' I asked.

'Man in black,' he mumbled through his swollen lips. He seemed to be missing at least a couple of teeth, too. 'Forced me off the road. Had a gun, but he didn't need it. Hit me with a tyre iron.'

'We'll get our own back,' I said, not caring

if the sheriff overheard. 'Don't you worry.'

'Sorry,' Jesse said. 'He made me talk. Asked about you and your plans. I had to tell him or he would have killed me. I could tell that from his eyes. That look we were talking about. He was a mean son of a bitch.'

Sirens sounded in the distance.

'You just rest up,' I said. 'I know he gave you no choice.'

The ambulance pulled up behind us and two paramedics rushed over. They took one look at Jesse and one of them went back for a stretcher. The other checked his pulse and seemed satisfied. One of the paramedics gave him a shot of some sort of painkiller, morphine maybe, immobilized his arm and then the two of them lifted him as gently as they could on to the stretcher, bringing a cry of pain from Jesse. They whisked him away and left us standing there, not knowing what to do next.

'They'll take him to the hospital in Reno, if you want to visit him.'

'What are you going to do about this man in black?' I asked.

'Keep an eye out for him,' Tucker answered.

'Keep both eyes out for him,' I said, 'and keep your gun handy. This guy is very dangerous. He may be out of your league.'

'But not out of yours,' he said, nodding his head. 'If you find him before me, that might be good. For all of us.'

I nodded. It was as near as he could go to give me carte blanche as to how I handled him. Tucker wasn't all bad after all. He could have the pieces after I'd dealt with the man in black.

* * *

The man in black's assault on Jesse altered things. By how much we couldn't know. I hadn't told Jesse much that would be useful to the man in black: what he knew was more about me rather than how we planned to fight the bikers, but we'd have to plan for the worst. We sat around the table drinking coffee and generally feeling depressed by the latest turn of events. There was no banter. The mood was solemn. Someone needed to break the silence.

'How much did Jesse know?' Bull asked.

'He didn't know the details of what we intended — the pit, the stinger and so on,' I said, 'but all the equipment he had on the truck would have told the man in black that something was going on. All we can do is stick to the plan and hope for the best. He doesn't know we've got a digger, so he might think we were just going to erect some sort of barricade with barbed wire.'

'Maybe I should just take his offer,' Red said, letting out a long sigh.

'Sell the ranch and move on?' I said, astounded.

'Might be best for all of us.'

'Start running and it becomes a habit,' I said. 'What will it take to make you back down next time? A little less? A lot less? What pride can you have in yourself? How can you stand tall?'

'We didn't bargain for this man in black. You said yourself that he was dangerous. Got the sheriff running scared, too.'

'We have to face him and beat him,' I said. 'He'll haunt all of us otherwise. Remember the Russians? We spent all those years looking over our shoulders, scared of any shadow. Tackle your enemy head on — that's the only way.'

Bull nodded. 'I agree with Johnny. Running's not the answer. Not for us. No one frightens me off by shooting a beer can and beating up a friend of mine.'

Pieter got up and went to the dresser, picked up a bottle of bourbon and five shot glasses. He poured out the bourbon and passed the glasses around. 'By rights, it should be gin,' he said. 'Dutch courage. I'm not looking forward to our next meeting with the man in black, but I'm not for running either. I can handle it. I vote we stay and face him.'

'There is an old saying in Poland,' Stan said. 'The sausage of the boar is sweeter than that of the pig.'

'And what the hell does that mean?' I asked.

'It means I agree with Pieter,' Stan said. 'What's life without some danger? We stay and fight. I'm not wasting all that planning. We face the man in black if we have to. Maybe if we put up a good show against the bikers, he'll back off.'

'Then we stay,' I said to Red.

They all nodded. The bottle of bourbon got passed around. The decision was made. I hoped it was the right one. I probably could have talked them out of staying if I'd wanted to. The responsibility was now mine.

'And so there's no doubt,' I said, 'the man in black is mine. No one touches him but me. There are scores to be settled.'

10

Pa Blenkenstein was right. Even though we were digging on the track, away from the foothills, it was hard work. You could almost hear the digger groan as you plunged the spikes of the bucket into the ground. The mound of earth by the side of the hole was increasing frustratingly slowly. This was going to take longer than we'd thought. It wasn't just digging the hole in the ground, it was getting rid of the material that we had dug out. We couldn't leave it by the trap or it would have been obvious that something wasn't right, so we had to use the digger to transfer the earth to a hiding-place behind the ranch house. At least we could use the earth to construct another firing position.

'This is going to take too long,' I said to Bull. 'Too much time ferrying earth around and too little digging.'

'It's gonna have to be manual labour,' he said. 'Spades and wheelbarrows. The digger digs and we transport.'

'Sounds like another trip to town. They're going to think we're building a whole new city at this rate.'

'Wouldn't be a bad idea, judging by the one they've got at the moment.'

'Don't deserve our custom.'

'Somehow I think that doesn't bother them.'

I nodded and went off to get the truck. I needed to talk to Jerome, so might as well kill two birds with one stone — neat trick if you can pull it off. Still doesn't beat shooting bits of twig.

I parked the truck outside the hardware store, told the bespectacled boy what I wanted and tipped him ten bucks to load everything for me. I crossed the street to where Jerome was in his usual place, rocking away with the dog by his side.

'Still here then,' he said.

'Looks like it,' I replied.

'Sure do,' he said.

'Beer?'

He nodded. 'And don't forget the peanuts.'

I obliged. Passed a beer to him and tested the dog's reflexes by flicking a peanut in the air for him to catch. He passed the test, although I didn't think he'd do that for much longer. He had that worn-out look that comes when your time approaches. He was going to leave a big hole in Jerome's life. Wouldn't seem the same, him rocking away on the porch without the dog.

I sipped my beer. 'What news from Jackson? Anything interesting on the senator?'

'Jackson reckons something's going down. Senator's more cagey than usual. All conversation stops whenever he comes in the room. Senator never used to bother — always treated Jackson as if he was deaf, dumb and blind, a non-person is what Jackson called it.'

'That doesn't surprise me.'

'Senator spends a lot of time with Slim — more so than usual, like they're cooking up something.'

'Did Jackson say anything about a man in black, drives a silver Mercedes?'

Jerome shook his head. 'If he'd come to the ranch house, then Jackson would have had to let him in. Would have mentioned it to me.' He looked up at me. 'What's with the man in black?'

'He don't seem to like us.'

'Lot of that going around.'

'If you see him, get out of his way. He's mean. Tried to buy Red's land and when that didn't work thought he could scare us off.'

'Gonna be a showdown coming?'

'Reckon so. He won't back off and neither will we.'

'Man in black ain't your only problem.'

I flicked another peanut in the air for the dog in a show of nonchalance. I raised an eyebrow at Jerome.

'Bikers are coming.'

'Tell me about it.'

'My sister works at a diner 'bout twenty miles from town. The bikers are camping out there. Numbers grow each day. They blab a lot, too. Gonna teach you a lesson, they say. Soon they'll be ready to take you on.'

'Anyone else who wants to join our enemies?'

'Not that I hear, but knowing you I wouldn't bank on it. Reckon trouble kinda follows you around.'

'Sometimes gets ahead of me, too.'

He nodded sagely.

'How about,' I said, 'visiting your sister for us? Take a look and report back to me. I'll give you fifty bucks and cover the costs of a meal.'

'Are you joking?'

'Deadly serious.'

'There speaks a man who's never had my sister's cooking. You only have to smell it for your arteries to clog. I'd stand more chance of surviving if I took on the bikers.'

'What about a hundred bucks and enough to cover a coffee.'

'Now you're talking. I'll skip the coffee, though — no better than her cooking.'

I wrote down my mobile number and gave it to him.

'Call me when you get back and we'll talk

over another beer.'

'Don't forget the dog.'

'Juicy steak do him?'

'Only if we cut it up small.'

'Nothing's too good for your dog.'

He reached down and patted the dog's head.

'Reckon so,' he said.

* * *

It was good to be doing some physical exercise again. Since arriving in Texas we'd spent a lot of time thinking and planning, and not enough grafting. Red was on mountain watch and the remaining four of us had stripped off our shirts in the afternoon sun. Like a well-oiled machine, we filled the wheelbarrows with spadefuls of earth and rock and trundled back and forth to a new mound we'd created behind the ranch house. Our bodies glistened with sweat and our muscles began to ache. It was a good workout.

I was impressed with Pieter. Since his early-morning training with Bull and a less calorific diet, he was getting fitter day by day. Soon we wouldn't have to worry about him letting us down when it came to the action.

We'd erected a barrier across the track so that no innocent person would stumble across our pit and fall in; it wouldn't make any difference to the bikers — they'd just kick it down and ride through. To their doom, we hoped.

As the sun started to set we ceased work for the day and went back to the ranch house to shower and start to relax as best we could. We assembled around the table to talk over progress and have a sundowner or two. Stan had set up a bar on an old side table and stocked it with various spirits, mixers, beer and a bucket of ice. He'd even managed to get some coasters so we didn't mark the table — not that with that old table anyone would have noticed. I helped myself to a long vodka and orange juice and sat down. Bull skipped the ice in his bourbon. Tooth no better, I thought.

'A good day's work,' I said.

'Be quicker tomorrow,' Bull said. 'Now that we have got a system in place.'

'If we start at sunrise,' Pieter said, 'do you reckon we can get finished tomorrow?'

I shook my head. 'Not if we're going to make it deep enough and wide enough to cause a real problem for the Angels. We're going to have to buy ourselves some time.'

Bull sipped at his beer and looked across the table at me. 'And how are we going to do that?'

'I've got a man working on it,' I said.

'There's maybe fifty bikers and you've got one man working on it!' Bull said.

'And his dog,' I said.

'And his dog,' Bull said with a shake of his head.

'I got to hand it to you, Johnny,' Red said. 'I admire your idea of fair odds.'

'We're doing the best we can to decrease the odds against us — the pit, the booby traps and so on — but we're still going to be heavily outnumbered. Unless . . . '

'Unless what?' Stan asked.

'Unless we whittle down the numbers against us. We need to get proactive.'

'Does that mean what I think it means?' said Bull.

'It do,' said Pieter.

'We're not going to sit here just waiting for the bikers to turn up,' I said. 'We're going to go to them. Catch them off guard. Take some of them out of the action.'

'And how are we going to do that,' Stan the strategist asked.

'I told you. I've got a man working on it.'

'And his dog,' Bull pointed out.

'They've set up camp at a diner twenty miles away. Jerome's going to case it out for me.'

'Jerome the old guy who sits outside the

hotel each day?' Red said, placing the ice cold beer can against his temple as if his brain was overheating.

'With his dog,' I said. 'Mustn't forget the dog.'

'Gonna make the world of difference,' Bull said, shaking his head.

'This is no ordinary dog,' I said. 'You should see him catch peanuts.'

Pieter jangled the ice around in his glass of bourbon. Looked at it for inspiration. 'Makes sense,' he said. 'Not the bit about the dog,' he hastened to add, 'but taking the fight to them. They're not going to be expecting that.'

'Always expect the unexpected,' Stan said unoriginally.

I wondered why he didn't have a Polish proverb for that. Probably best not to ask. He'd only say something incomprehensible about grandma's soup always tasting better when eaten with a fork.

'Early start tomorrow, guys,' I said, getting up from the table.

'And what's different about that?' Pieter said.

'Don't blame me,' Bull said. 'You shouldn't have allowed yourself to get out of shape so quickly.'

'Well I didn't expect to be facing fifty bikers, did I?'

'Maybe it won't be fifty after tomorrow,' I said.

'Why do you always have to spoil it by saying 'maybe'?' Bull asked.

'Because I'm naturally cautious. It's a philosophy that's always served me well. But no, not maybe. We'll find a way of whittling down the numbers. I trust my old-timer.'

'And his dog,' Red said.

'Dog's gonna make all the difference,' Bull said. 'We can't lose.'

'Amen to that,' I said.

11

I let go of the handles of the wheelbarrow and stretched my back. The sun was relentless and I wiped some sweat off my brow. It was noon and we had been working since seven o'clock that morning. At last we were making some real progress. The hole was now about three feet deep and measured ten feet square. It was our first line of defence; I hoped it would catch us a good few bikers and make some others take us seriously: maybe quit. Maybe. I took a swallow of my water bottle to wash away the dust we were generating from the digger. In the distance I could see three riders on horseback. As they got closer, I recognized them as Fey, Cameron and Lucy. I strolled over to meet them so that they wouldn't get too near to the hole and guess our plans. You can't be too careful. Lucy dismounted first and grabbed my hand, looking up at me with dreamy eyes. Since rescuing her from the bolting horse, I suspected I had become sort of knight in shining armour for her — hard act to live up to. Cameron latched on to Red: two half-caste Native Americans together.

'To what do we owe the pleasure of this visit?' I asked.

Fey came across and kissed my cheek. 'I've got some news,' she said. 'We've had an offer to buy the Retreat. Arrived in the post this morning.'

'Who's the would-be buyer?' I asked.

'We don't know. The letter was from some hotshot law firm in Odessa: Crane, Oaks and Crane. They said it was 'on behalf of an interested party'. We'd like to ask your advice on what to do. We're having a meeting tonight and would like you to come along. Do say yes.'

I had other plans for tonight, but they would have to wait for the cover of darkness. And this news seemed a bit too coincidental. 'I'd love to come. Can I be away by seven?'

'We'll start at six and it shouldn't take more than an hour — the offer is the only thing we need to discuss as a group.'

'What are you doing?' asked Lucy, pointing at the pile of earth that was waiting for us to transport it out of sight.

'Just some work on the track,' I said. 'You might say we're preparing it for some vehicles. Best you go the long way to the ranch house next time you come. Or come round the back — we've taken a post-and-rail down so that we can easily move between our place and the Retreat.'

'Oh,' Lucy said. She looked pensive. 'Are you married?'

I stood there in shock. 'Not exactly,' I said.

'How can you be 'not exactly' married?' she asked.

'It's just that we haven't got around to it yet.'

'So is it like being engaged?'

I nodded.

'So you're like a family?'

I nodded again.

'I've always wanted a proper family. Can I come and live with you? I'm grown-up for my age. I could help you with whatever you do.'

'I run a bar. It's not the kind of work that's suitable for a young lady like you.'

'Well, I could help you out at home — sweep the floors, tidy up, cook your meals. Whatever. Please let me stay with you.'

'I live on a small island. There's no proper school and a girl your age needs a solid education so you can do whatever you please when you grow up.'

'You don't want me, do you?' she said. I could feel she was on the brink of tears. 'You don't like me.'

'No, that's not right. Of course, I like you — you're a lovely girl. But life on the island is different — there's no riding horses for a start. And there's Anna to consider — she's my, er, lady. I don't think it would work, especially as we're having a baby.'

'You're having a baby! It was supposed to be my family. That you'd look after me. That I'd belong. But it won't be like that. You'll spend all your time mooning over some dumb baby.' She let go of my hand and turned to Fey. 'Let's go,' she said. She turned to me. 'And don't think you're sitting next to me at this meeting.'

She stamped her foot, turned her back to me and mounted her pony.

'See you at six,' Fey said, smiling.

I nodded. There was a lot of thinking to do before then.

Bull came across to stand beside me. 'Mighty big coincidence,' he said.

'That's what I was thinking. We need to know more about this deal and the hotshot law firm.'

'And whether one of them knows the man in black.'

'Exactly.'

* * *

I broke off from wheelbarrow duty at four o'clock, showered, changed and went into town. Jerome had called earlier and said I needed to see him in person, not just on the telephone.

When I arrived he was actually showing someone to their room in the hotel. I went to the gunsmith's first, bought silencers for all of us, then went back to the hotel. He ushered me inside and took me into the bar area.

He led me to a table in the corner where we could watch anyone coming in. The bar had a lot of wood panelling to waist height, a long highly polished counter with high stools so that lonely folk could talk to the barman, wooden tables and chairs around the perimeter. The dog wasn't allowed inside so he stayed dozing on the porch.

I bought two beers and, for later, a bowl of peanuts. Jerome spread a large sheet of paper over the table.

'This is the diner,' he said, pointing to a pencilled rectangle in the middle of the paper. 'The bikers are camped to the east of it. According to my sister, after having a meal in the diner they gather round a big campfire and swap stories and drink, maybe smoke a little grass. There are about twenty of them now, too many for the small diner to accommodate all of them in one sitting. Not that there are many other customers — the bikers have scared them all off. They sleep in tents spread around the warmth of the fire.' He pointed to some triangles on the right-hand side of the small circle that represented the fire. 'Maybe if you leave it till about midnight, they will all be stoned on something or other.'

'Where do they park the bikes?'

'They're lined up outside the front entrance to the diner so that they can see them in the light from the windows.'

'What time does the diner close?'

'Used to be around nine in the evening, but the bikers changed all that. Now it closes when they say so.' He shrugged. 'No regular pattern, my sister says. She's just thankful that they don't make trouble. And, of course, it's all extra money. In some ways the diner has never had it so good. Done more meals than they ever had in the past.'

'Is there anywhere we can park the jeep so it can't be seen?'

'The diner is on a bend. If you stop short of the bend, there's a clump of trees. You will be out of view there.'

I nodded. A plan was forming. Risky, given the odds, but I fancied it to work.

We sipped our beer. I gave Jerome the promised hundred-dollar bill.

'Where does your sister live?' I asked. 'Not the diner, presumably.'

'She lives in a mobile home about a quarter of a mile away.'

'Call her and tell her to stay inside tonight

— that's if they let her close up early. There's going to be some action.'

He nodded. 'Look after yourself,' he said. 'There's a lot of them and they won't take too kindly to whatever you plan. I'd rather like to see you sitting next to me on the porch tomorrow. And don't forget the steak. Dog's looking forward to it — don't let him down.'

'Don't worry, old timer. I'm a hard guy to get rid of. I'll meet you here in the morning.'

'God willing,' he said.

'Reckon so.'

* * *

On the way back I stopped at the grocery store for a crate of beer and some sugar, then called at the gas station. I already had the silencers I'd bought from the gun shop — the proprietor must have thought Christmas and Thanksgiving had come all on one day since our arrival. I just about had enough time to unload, pick up Red and drive to the Retreat for six o'clock. I gave Jerome's map to Stan and told him my basic idea — he could put the finishing touches to it. We agreed that our aim was 'shock and awe'. The bikers wouldn't know what hit them.

The residents were already seated at the long table when we arrived. They'd kept two seats for Red and me and the rest of the people were standing up clustered around the walls. Red sat with Cameron and I was positioned next to Fey. Lucy, as far away from me as possible, looked across at me and poked her tongue out. I felt like a heel. Maybe I should have played along with the game a bit, but I didn't want her to take anything too seriously. I looked away from Lucy and across to Cameron. Her eyes were red: she'd been crying.

'What's the matter?' asked Red.

'Some people at my school call me names. They say I'm not as good as them because I'm half Red Indian.'

'That's true,' Red said. 'You're not as good as them.' He smiled at her. 'You're better. Much better. We Native Americans were the original inhabitants of these lands. Our roots go back thousands of years. Unfortunately for the kids at your school, their history only spans a few hundred years. We have heritage, you and I, and that takes a long time to get. We can be proud of what we are. We are noble.'

She smiled at him. 'Wait till I get back to school. I'll put them in their place, those palefaces.' She looked at me. 'No offence,' she said.

'None taken,' I replied.

Her face took on a pensive look, then she looked up at Red. 'I know you're a Comanche — and that's not as good as Cheyenne — but I'd like to know more of our history. Will you teach me?'

'You betcha. Give me a week to sort out a few issues surrounding the ranch and we'll get started. Comanche brave teachum littlum Cheyenne squaw.'

Cameron beamed at him and squeezed his hand.

Rafael stood up and clapped his hands. A hush came over the room.

'My friends,' he said. 'My friends of the Retreat and my neighbours who are friends, too. Welcome. Welcome to our humble house.' His voice became grave. 'We are gathered here because we face a life-changing decision. Do we stay or go.'

I interrupted his flow. We needed some cold hard facts to balance the emotion. 'What have you been offered for the land?'

'A million dollars,' Rafael said.

'About what it's worth, a little less maybe,' said Red. 'The offer for mine was two million dollars and my spread is twice as big as yours. Seems a fair price.'

'I agree,' said Rafael. 'I paid six hundred thousand for it out of my inheritance from my grandfather only a couple of years ago.

But this is not just about money. This is our home. Do we want to give up what we have built here?'

A hand went in the air and Rafael nodded approval.

'Where would we go?' a young man asked.

'Somewhere easier, I hope,' an old man said. 'The land here ain't right for farming. Steers, yes — but we ain't cowboys. Not good for the sort of crops we want. It breaks my back.'

There were nods of agreement around the table.

Cameron put her hand up and Rafael nodded.

'I like it here,' she said. 'I like riding the horses, the open spaces, watching the eagles in the foothills of the mountains. I don't mind the work; I guess we all have to do some work and the time passes quickly. I vote to stay, and if you decide to move, then I'll ask Red if I can live with him. I'm a good rider — as good as any man, and I can help round up the cattle. Maybe cooking, too. Whatever. I won't be a burden.'

'That's a big commitment you're making for someone else,' I said. 'Maybe you should talk to Red about it before making any decision.'

'I can live with that,' said Red. 'It would be

good to have a youngster around.' He looked her in the eye. 'You'd have to teach me about how to be a good parent, I've got no experience of that. But it could work.'

Wow! That was some responsibility he was prepared to take on. I wondered if he would feel the same later when the sentimental home-loving atmosphere of the meeting was over. And when we were going to do things that night that might get us into trouble and certainly wouldn't set a good example. Or maybe it would. Fight for what you believe in.

A young woman with flaxen hair in pigtails and a baby on her lap spoke up. 'This is the place where I want to bring up our kids. The air is clean, the weather good, lots of space for them to roam around safely. I've got attached to it. I know we're not popular in the town — long-haired hippies, they call us with scorn — and the senator would like to see the back of us, but we can keep trying to change their minds. This is our home. I'd like to stay.'

There were some murmurings of agreement from around the table. The old man who had spoken earlier shook his head and rubbed his back to emphasize his view.

'I think it's time we had an impartial view,' said Rafael. 'What do you think, Johnny?'

Nothing like being put on the spot.

'I suppose,' I said, playing for a little time, 'that the decision depends mainly on money. You take their offer, buy somewhere else and have some money to put in the bank. The big question is: do you need the money? You have a community here and that shouldn't be underrated. You have a simple life. You don't seem to want for anything here — food on your plates and roofs over your heads. You have a lifestyle many would envy. What would you spend the money on? How would your life be improved?'

'I guess it would be there to fall back on in hard times,' Rafael said.

'That's what neighbours are for,' said Red.

'It's your money,' I said to Rafael. 'The choice should be yours. What do you say?'

'I say that we're a democratic group here. Let's put it to the vote.'

'One last thing,' I said. 'Someone tried to buy Red's land and when that didn't work they tried to frighten us off. The same might happen to you if you turn down the offer. Someone wants this land badly. It might not be worth a fight for you, and you're a far easier target than Red and we are. Things could get sticky, to say the least.'

'Will you help us if it comes to a fight?' Rafael asked.

'To be honest,' I said, 'we're pretty

stretched as it is.' I looked questioningly at Red. He nodded. 'But we'll be there if you need us. I promise you we won't abandon you.'

'Then let's vote,' said Rafael. 'All those who want to stay, raise your hands. And now all those who want to sell up and move on, raise your hands.'

It was around a two-to-one majority for staying. The die was cast. I only hoped we could live up to our promise. Come to think of it, I only hoped we wouldn't have to.

12

We decided to play it safe and not leave the ranch until one o'clock in the morning. There followed a long debate over who should go and who should stay on guard. Everyone wanted to be involved in the attack and in the end we reckoned that at that time in the morning we were pretty safe not to have to leave anyone behind.

As this was night time we donned our dark clothing and the four of us bar Bull, for whom it was unnecessary, buddied up to smear each other's faces with dark camouflage make-up: Red went for the full war-paint look with stripes along each cheek. I hate to admit it, but we were starting to look the business. If I met one of us in the dark, I'd be scared.

We stowed our handguns in the shoulder holsters — silencers not yet fitted since it would make drawing the guns slower — loaded up the jeep with the assault rifles and our secret weapons, then we all squeezed inside. We drove for about forty minutes and parked where Jerome had indicated. It was further away than was ideal, but we'd just have to lug the equipment to the diner.

It was just like Jerome had described. If I needed a mapmaker in the future, then I'd choose him. The lights of the diner were still on and the white weatherboarding stood out against the backdrop of the hills. The light being on was a nuisance: it shone directly on the rows of around twenty bikes. There was a glow from the campfire, but everywhere else was pitch black. But in that glow we could see two seated figures, backs to us, around the campfire. They had to be our first target.

We were just about to launch our attack when I noticed a figure moving in the diner. It was a stout black lady whom I assumed to be Jerome's sister. Surely she should have shut up hours ago, but it wasn't she who was calling the shots: if the bikers wanted you open, then you did what they said and stayed open.

'Stay here,' I said to the others. 'Don't start anything until I have the black woman out and the lights go off. Once she is safe, we hit them.'

I headed out of range of the light and crept along parallel to the diner. When I was past it I circled around to the far side and peeked through the window. Chairs had been placed upside down on the tables and the black woman was mopping the floor. I had to get her attention. Then I realized the snag. If the woman saw me, she'd freak out — a warpainted warrior peering through the window would scare the life out of her. She'd scream her head off and alert the bikers. If that happened we would soon be surrounded. The biter bit. Mincemeat of five mercenaries.

I let out a deep sigh — my breath came out in a cloud. That gave me the idea.

I went very close to the window and breathed on the glass. I didn't know how long the condensation would last so I wrote quickly, which is not easy to do when you're writing backwards so that the letters come out in the right order for the viewer. I wrote just three words in block capitals — JEROME OPEN UP. I tapped as loud as I dared on the window and then crouched out of view.

No reaction.

I blew another stream on to the window to revitalize the letters and tapped more loudly this time. I checked the two men around the fire and they hadn't moved.

A shadow came through the window. It was motionless for a few seconds and then disappeared from view. I heard the sound of the lock turning in the door and edged towards it. The door swung open and I jumped inside. I grabbed the woman around the waist from the back so that she couldn't see my face and put my left hand over her mouth.

'I'm a friend,' I said. 'Friend of Jerome. Johnny. You're safe with me. Keep calm. Now I going to take my hand away from your mouth. Please don't scream. Nod your head if you understand,'

She nodded. I took my hand away and let out the breath I had been holding. She turned around and let out a gasp when she saw my face.

'What do you want?' she said, her voice tinged with fear.

'We're planning a little party for the bikers,' I said. 'I need to get you away from here. Somewhere safe.'

She nodded again, still not over her panic on seeing me.

'In a moment I want you to turn the lights off and we're both going to step through the door. Can you manage to run?'

'Sure can,' she said, calming down a little now. 'Like the hounds of hell are after me.'

'That may be nearer the truth than either of us would want. OK, lights off.'

She reached to a panel behind the door and flicked switches to turn off several banks of fluorescent lights inside the diner. They flickered and died.

I took hold of her and guided her outside. 'OK, run,' I said.

'Follow me.'

I checked that the two men around the fire were still looking the other way, took hold of her hand and we ran in a straight line back to the others.

She stared at them for a while. 'Name's Marsha, by the way. Good job you're friends,' she said. 'I wield a killer mop.'

'Where do you live?' I said.

'Back down the road a mile. Fifteen-minute walk.'

'OK,' I said. I pointed in the other direction. 'Back a way down the road you'll see a jeep. Sit there and wait for us and we'll take you home. You'll hear a lot of loud noises. Just stay where you are and you'll be fine.'

'Whatever you're going to do, good luck,' she said and walked away down the road.

I motioned to Bull and Pieter and pointed my finger at the two men seated around the fire. Fortunately, they were sitting next to each other rather than facing, which meant that both Bull and Pieter could approach the men from behind and not be noticed. We'd been through this sort of scenario while rehearsing the plan. Bull and Pieter drew their guns and crept up to the fire. One blow to each man's head was enough to knock them out and remove them from the action. They grabbed the men under the arms and dragged them back to the safety of the trees — our preference was to get away without any severe casualties. *Shock and awe*. Phase 1 complete.

Red and I drew our handguns and fitted the silencers. We went across to the diner. Our first target was the engines. Red went to the far end of the line and I took the nearer end. We opened the petrol caps and poured sugar inside the tanks. The sugar would gum up the works and the engines would be dead. A great way to immobilize a vehicle without showing any visible signs.

We next worked back along the line, firing shots at both tyres of every bike; they could not now be ridden until fitted with new tyres, and the chances of getting forty or fifty spares in one go were low. Phase 2 complete.

Now for the fun. Bull and I spread out so that we were at opposite sides facing the tents. Time for Pieter, Red and Stan to take centre stage. I saw three lighters shine brightly in the darkness and that was the cue for Bull and me. We opened fire with our assault rifles, spraying the ground in front of the tents and making loads of noise. Then the Molotov cocktails started raining down.

The campsite was awash with light now. Men in their underwear started to crawl out of the short narrow openings of the tents, saw what was happening and ran in panic towards the woods. Wherever they ran, a Molotov cocktail followed them. We kept throwing till the men had disappeared in the distance and every tent was ablaze. Third and final phase complete. Time to head for the hills.

We abandoned the empty beer crate and the packets of sugar, sprayed one last volley of bullets from our assault rifles and ran as quickly as we could back to the jeep.

'You take Marsha back home, Red. We'll start walking and you can pick us up on the way back,' I said.

He held the door open for Marsha, jumped into the front seat and sped off into the distance.

We started walking. The absence of light kept us to a slow pace, but that didn't matter — there was no danger from the bikers and it would only be a few minutes before Red picked us up.

We saw the headlights in the distance and stepped into the cover of some trees until we were sure it was the jeep. Red brought the jeep, brakes full on, to a halt beside us and we climbed inside.

He drove us back at breakneck speed and,

adrenaline pumping through our veins, we collapsed with laughter into the chairs around the table. Charged up as we were, there would be little sleep tonight. We poured ourselves a drink and toasted each other.

'Well done, Stan,' I said. 'Everything went according to plan. I'd like to see those bikers' faces in the morning when they realize that they have no belongings except the underwear they slept in, and then see what we did to the bikes. I think we've bought ourselves the time we need. And I'd also be surprised if some of those bikers didn't turn tail and run.'

'Sure showed them we were no pushover,' Bull said. 'Been a while since I had such fun.'

'Beats a safari every day,' said Pieter, giving a big grin.

'I'd like to see the face of the man in black when he hears the news,' said Red. 'Wonder what he will do then?'

'Somehow we need to track him down,' I said, 'or at least get him to come to us. The bikers are a threat because of their numbers — and after tonight they won't hold back when they hit us — but the man in black can afford to wait and pick us off one by one, if necessary. If he kills Red, maybe he'll think we'd have no reason to stick around.'

'Thanks for that comforting thought,' Red said gravely.

'We need another plan,' said Stan. 'I'll start working on it in the morning. Can't think straight at the moment. Need to rid my head of tonight and all the excitement.'

I downed my first vodka and poured another.

'You do realize what we've done?' I said.

All eyes at the table turned to me.

'What?' Bull said.

'After tonight there can be no turning back. Our enemies will double their efforts. We have to see this thing through to the bitter end.'

'Bring them on,' Pieter said.

'Yeah, bring 'em on,' echoed Bull.

'Hell,' I said. 'Reckon so.'

* * *

The sheriff came just after nine in the morning. We broke off the digging to watch him walking along the track, seeing that his car couldn't get through our barricade. I suspected that would only exacerbate a bad mood.

'What are you boys up to?' he asked. 'Seems like you're always up to something.'

'Can't have idle hands,' I said. 'Makes work for the devil.'

'We had us a bit of a ruckus,' he said. 'At

the diner. Someone did a pretty good job of scaring the bikers. They've got nothing to wear and their bikes were sabotaged. Wouldn't know anything about it, would you? What were you boys up to around one thirty in the morning?'

'That's the time we have our sewing circle,' I said. 'Idle hands, remember?'

'I might have known I wouldn't get a straight answer.' He took off his hat and wiped his brow with the back of his hand. ''Course I'm mighty riled up that someone could come into my territory and upset those nice biker boys. Almost cried in my coffee when I heard about it.'

'Understandable,' I said. 'Them being such good role models for the youth of today.'

He nodded. 'That too,' he said. He looked around at the digging. 'Expecting any more trouble?'

'Nothing we can't handle,' I said.

'That I can believe,' he said. 'Mighty big pit you're digging. Gonna be deep enough?'

'We hope so. But, if not, we've got a few more tricks up our sleeves.'

'That I can believe, too.' He frowned. 'This is a pretty thin line you're treading. Don't fall on the wrong side or I might have to show you that mean side of me. Only got room for two in my cells, so I won't be taking any prisoners. Understand me, boys?'

'Crystal-clear, Sheriff,' I said. 'We're both on the same side.'

'Make sure you remember that.'

'Oh, and Sheriff,' I said. 'We'd rather you didn't tell anyone about the pit.'

He put his hat back on, turned around and said as he walked off, 'What pit?'

13

It was time for a bit of metaphorical digging as opposed to the real stuff. Our best clue as to what was going on was the letter to Rafael containing the offer to purchase his property. It was time we went to see the legal hotshots: Crane, Oaks & Crane.

Red and I set off early in the jeep, stopped at the Retreat to pick up the letter and headed out on Route 20 to Odessa. It was just short of a hundred miles, which would be covered pretty quickly with Red driving — if luck was on our side and we actually got there in one piece, that is.

When we got to the town of Pyote — about a third of the way there — I spotted a café that was advertising fresh doughnuts. I told Red to stop and we went inside. It was a small place with red-check tablecloths and pine chairs. There was hardly a seat to be had, which spoke well for the place, and, hopefully, for the quality of the doughnuts. There was a heated cabinet displaying a whole variety of them. I got myself a bag and, using the tongs provided, got a mixture, eight in all. To this we added coffee in paper cups and paid the lady behind the counter. When we got back to the jeep I handed Red the bag and the coffees.

'You eat and drink and I'll drive for a while.'

He looked at me suspiciously, then took a look inside the bag of doughnuts, weakened, and nodded. He climbed into the passenger seat and started eating. I drove off at normal speed and listened to him munching. The doughnuts smelt good, but they could wait till we next stopped.

'Tell me about this poker game,' I said to Red. 'Did you risk all the money we made in Amsterdam?'

'Wasn't no risk involved,' he said. 'I knew I had him beat.'

'Must have been a pretty big bet,' I said.

'The guy who owned the ranch was in hock to the bank for the mortgage. He was struggling with the payments and was getting desperate. He called a high-stakes game and hoped to win enough money to solve all his problems, or at least buy him some time with the bank. He was a lousy poker player when he was sober, but he'd been drinking and that made his judgement unreliable. I knew if the cards fell for me I could clean up.'

He took a sip of his coffee and rolled it round in his mouth, savouring the flavour, before swallowing it.

'We were playing seven-card stud. I've got two queens in the hole and two more queens and a ten face up. Don't get that kind of hand too often. His face cards were two jacks and a deuce — the most he could have was four jacks and I beat that. He must have thought I was bluffing, or maybe he didn't see the significance of my face cards, just kept pushing the money in till he had nothing left on the table. Said he'd back his hand with the ranch, less the mortgage.

'I could get the cash to cover that bet — hadn't hardly touched the money we made in Amsterdam. I called him and he laid down his cards, full house, jacks on deuces, smiling all the time. I faced my cards and he slumped back in his chair.

'The ranch and all the land was mine, provided I could keep up with the mortgage payments — and that wasn't a problem. I could use the Amsterdam money for that while I built up the business so that it was profitable. He handed me the deeds the next morning. Then he shot himself that night. Put a bit of a dampener on things.'

'I can imagine,' I said. 'Did he have any family or anyone who might want revenge on you? Could be another reason why you've got all this trouble.'

Red shook his head. 'He was a loner — no family. Wasn't popular either — was a loudmouth as well as a drunk. I doubt there'd be anyone who would want to get even.'

'Promise me you won't do anything as stupid again. No big risks. You've got the chance of a good life here — don't spoil it.'

He gave a non-committal grunt.

'Get a good adrenaline rush playing poker. Hard feeling to beat. I was pretty high when we got back from Amsterdam. Poker was a way of getting some of that excitement back.'

We were coming to the outskirts of Odessa. I pulled the jeep over.

'Your turn to drive,' I said. 'Can't resist those doughnuts any longer.'

I got out, stretched my legs and went round to the passenger seat. Red stepped out and I took his place. I chose a cinnamon doughnut and took a bite. Something about America: the only place where you can get a decent doughnut.

Red made to pull off.

'Not yet,' I said. 'I need to be serious and I can't do that while you're driving — takes all my attention just praying.'

'You gonna lecture me?' Red said.

'Seems like you may have more responsibilities in the future. Not just for the farm and your workers, but for Cameron, too, if that's what the gods have in store for you. You need to set a good example from now on.'

'Did I do the right thing?' he asked. 'About Cameron?'

'Seems a good kid,' I said. 'She could do worse having you as a surrogate father or even just a mentor. You've got good principles, know the difference between right and wrong and don't blur the edges when it suits you. Not qualities you find in every man. Don't mess this up by doing anything stupid. She'll look up to you. Don't let her down.'

'I won't,' he said. 'I promise. You know it's good to have someone to whom you can belong.'

'To whom?' I said. 'Comanches getting good at English grammar.'

'Gonna have to get good at a whole host of things if I'm gonna teach Cameron.'

'Have the right attitude and the rest will come.'

I finished the doughnut, took a sip of cold coffee, winced, and wiped the sugar away from my mouth. 'Let's go,' I said. 'See what the hotshot lawyers have to say.'

'What do you call fifty lawyers at the bottom of the ocean?' Red asked.

I shook my head.

'A start,' he said.

* * *

Crane, Oaks & Crane was situated on the top floor of a modern five-storey building in town. There was a lot of glass at the front so that those workers high enough up the food chain to have an office could look down at the people walking along the street below. Maybe it went some way to compensate for being cooped up behind a desk all day, though I doubted it.

We walked up the stairs rather than put ourselves at the mercy of the lift — old habits die hard — and came out into a lobby with a receptionist sitting behind a polished-oak desk; maybe the oak was obligatory. Probably a room with a crane in it, too. The receptionist looked up at us as we entered. Didn't seem impressed. Probably not used to two guys in faded denim jeans and T-shirts. Red had on his favourite cowboy boots; she didn't seem to change her expression: raised eyebrows over black-rimmed spectacles. She was wearing a white blouse with one button too many undone, presenting us with a view of breasts I reckoned she was pretty proud of. I couldn't see under the desk, but I guessed at a pencil skirt an inch too short. Only fair. If she was going to make judgements about us from our appearance, then we could do the same.

'Can I help you, gentlemen?' she asked.

I could see that it caused her discomfort to call us gentlemen. I took the letter out of my pocket and slid it across her desk. 'We're here to see Mr Crane,' I said.

'Which one?' she asked.

'Whichever one wrote this letter,' I said. 'There are some initials at the bottom.'

She scrutinized the letter. 'That will be Mr Crane junior,' she said. 'Do you have an appointment?'

This was the tricky part. 'Not exactly,' I said.

'What does that mean?' she said frowning. If she'd put us down as troublemakers, she was applauding herself at this point.

'It means that Mr Crane junior will want to see us. Show him the letter and tell him we need to talk the offer through. Might win you a brownie point for showing initiative — always assuming that's encouraged here.'

I walked across to two steel-framed chairs and sat down. Nodded at Red who did the same. The receptionist sighed and thought about what to do. Should she follow my lead and leave reception unmanned? Call Mr Crane or his secretary and try to explain the situation while we were listening in? Call Security and have us kicked out? I could hear cogs in her brain whirring.

'Wait here,' she said, getting up from her desk. I congratulated myself — it *was* a pencil skirt — black — but slightly higher than I'd thought. It was just about decent and she smoothed it down, subconsciously trying to make it longer. That was one battle she wasn't going to win.

She walked through a set of glass doors and we could see her going through an open-plan office to a door at the end of the building. She emerged a couple of minutes later, opened the glass doors and signalled to us to follow. Faces looked up as we walked past, trying to guess what business we had there — needing help to get out of a murder rap, perhaps. She knocked on the door and immediately opened it. She made an economical arm movement for us to enter.

A man in his forties stood up to greet us. He was wearing a dark-blue suit with a light pinstripe: it signalled conservative, but with a hint of individuality. To go with the suit was a light-blue shirt with a button-down collar and a blue-and-red striped tie. He had on black loafers with a gold buckle. He had us well beat on the sartorial front. But after that there wasn't much going for him.

He was maybe thirty pounds overweight, an athlete's body — football player? — where the muscle had gone to fat. His face had the red tinge of someone who is a habitual drinker. His hair was grey and receding badly. And to top it all was a long, straight nose that was twice the size he needed in order to breathe.

'Gentlemen,' he said. 'Take a seat. Can I offer you something? Coffee?'

We gave him our coffee orders and sat down to wait for its arrival. It came in black mugs that wouldn't show the grounds. It was good, though. Freshly made from a good bean: Arabica, I reckoned.

'We'd like to know some more detail about this offer. Talk us through it please.'

'It's all quite clear,' he said. 'One million dollars for the land and all its buildings. The buyer would like completion within the next fortnight.' He smiled at us as if he was talking to a pair of idiots.

'What's the buyer going to do with the land?' I asked.

'Ranch it, I presume,' he said.

'You presume?' I said. 'Someone comes to you with a deal for a million dollars and all you're left with is a presumption?'

'I'm not sure that what the buyer wants the land for is relevant,' he said.

'There's neighbours involved,' said Red. 'Wouldn't want them inconvenienced or the value of their land to plummet because someone's going to open a trailer park for drug-takers out on probation.'

He thought about this for a while. Didn't seem to come to any conclusion.

'All you need to do is sell. If I were you, I wouldn't concern myself with neighbours.'

Red shook his head as if he didn't like what was going down.

'And who is the buyer?' I asked.

'The buyer is a recently formed real estate company. Could be they want the land as a sound investment.'

'And the name of this company?' Red said.

'Blue Valley Developments Inc,' Mr Crane replied.

'And who owns the company?' I asked.

'That is none of your business,' he answered. He didn't seem to like the way the conversation was going. 'I'll prepare the papers and you just sign — it's as easy as that.'

'If Blue Valley is a bona fide company, then I assume we could look up who runs it from their filed accounts,' I said. 'So why don't you just tell us? Save us the trouble of doing our research.'

'Drop it,' he said. 'You'll save yourself time and trouble.'

'We're used to both those things,' I said. 'Isn't that right, Red?'

'Reckon so,' he said and looked Crane in the eye.

Crane started to look flustered. 'As I said, drop it. It won't do you any good. In this state, you're right, a new company does have to file its accounts, including information on its shareholders.'

'Well, then, tell us,' said Red.

'It has to file those accounts within nine months of the end of its financial year. As it's a recently formed company that means you've got about twenty months to wait.'

He looked smug. He wasn't going to tell, short of us pulling out our guns and pinning him to the wall with the barrels stabbing his forehead. That would have been Bull's preference, but we had to tread a bit more lightly here. My bet was that Crane knew the local police, probably on first-name terms. He'd scream if we tried to force the issue and we'd finish up behind bars.

'We don't seem to be getting very far, Mr Crane,' I said. 'I can see your problem about client confidentiality. Why don't you just put the relevant file on your desk and go out and use the men's room? You wouldn't be breaking any rules and you might just persuade us to sell. Client would be pleased then, wouldn't he?'

'I'm going to give you ten seconds to leave

this office or I phone Security.'

Security wouldn't thank him for that. Would need to be a lot of them and they'd take a beating.

'Make your choice, gentlemen,' he said, reaching for the phone.

I stood up and Red followed my example.

'I won't shake your hand, Crane,' I said. 'Probably got the taint of dirty money on it.'

I turned on my heel and we walked out, passing the same bewildered faces looking up from their computers. The receptionist heaved a sigh of relief when we walked past her, or maybe she was just trying to give us a final view of her heaving chest.

'Didn't learn much,' said Red.

'On the contrary,' I said. 'We know that whoever is behind Blue Valley wants to keep it a secret. Got to be up to something. All we need to do is figure out what.'

We reached the jeep. 'You drive,' I said. 'I've got some thinking to do, and I do that best with my eyes closed.'

* * *

We got back in time for lunch. Pieter was on watch on the hills and Stan and Bull were dusty and caked with sweat from wheelbarrow duty. Ho, ably assisted by what seemed to be a doting Stan, brought in two large plates of sandwiches, two jars of dill pickles, some beers and bottled water. She anxiously asked if two jars of pickles would be enough: Stan smiled proudly.

It was while I was eating that the idea came to me.

'It's time we had a little excursion,' I said to Bull and Red. 'I think we might mosey out and see our favourite senator. It's time you two got acquainted properly.'

'This wouldn't have anything to do with getting out of wheelbarrow duty, would it?' said Red.

'Perish the thought,' I said. 'We need information and I've got a hunch the senator might provide us with some.'

'Won't it kinda rile him up, seeing Bull? said Red.

'That's what I'm hoping.'

Bull and I showered and changed into some clean clothes.

'Must make a good impression,' I said to Bull.

'How are we going to play this?' he asked. 'What's the plan?'

'As Red said, we're going to rile him up.'

'It's what we do best,' he said. 'Why change the habit of a lifetime?'

* * *

'So remind me of your grand plan,' said Red.

We were sitting in the jeep outside the main gates to the senator's ranch.

'We're going to get him angry,' I said.

'That's easy for you,' Bull said. 'You have a natural talent for that. But what about me? What role do I play?'

'You're going to be the catalyst.'

'Does the catalyst get to shoot anybody?'

'Not this time. Maybe on another occasion.'

'How about punching anybody?'

'Nope.'

'You're not playing to my talents,' Bull said, shaking his head.

'Just being there is going to be enough. Trust me.'

'Then I'll be there real good.'

We cruised up the driveway and parked outside the house. It was quiet. We got out and looked around. Not much action. Yet. I rang the doorbell and waited for Jackson. Bull stood beside me, humming a tune I didn't recognize. Something told me he was going to enjoy this.

The door opened and Jackson looked up at us. He frowned at Bull.

'We've come to see the senator,' I said.

'I'll see if he is at home,' Jackson said.

He turned his back and started to walk along the hall. We followed one step behind.

'You can't do that, sirs,' he said in panic. 'You must wait at the door. That's how it works.'

'If we do that the senator won't be at home. You know that, Jackson. He might deign to see me, Red at a push even, but Bull here doesn't stand a chance.' I gave him a reassuring smile. 'Don't worry, we'll see you don't get into trouble. Now lead on.'

He sighed and continued to walk towards the back of the house. He stopped at the last door on the left and knocked. We turned the handle and went inside before O'Hara could answer.

This was obviously his study. He was sitting on a large brown leather swivel-chair at an antique partners' desk with an inlaid green leather top. The size of the desk meant that it dominated the room. Along one wall were book-shelves lined with leather-bound tomes that I bet had never been opened — might even be fake for all I knew. There was a portrait of the senator on the wall facing the desk, so that O'Hara could look up from the desk and bask in the radiant smile the painter had somehow managed to create on his lips. O'Hara looked up and started to go purple with rage. Jackson stood nervously by the door.

'Before you explode,' I said, 'don't blame Jackson. We barged our way in.'

'How dare you,' he said. 'If it wasn't bad enough you coming,' he pointed at Bull, 'but to bring that man . . . '

'That man has a name. I'm called Bull. Remember that the next time you speak to me.'

'Get Slim,' O'Hara said to Jackson.

Jackson looked at me questioningly.

'Go on,' I said.

Bull moved back to the wall to the right of the door. Leaned back casually with his arms crossed over his chest.

'What do you want?' O'Hara said. He sounded more confident now that Jackson had left to get Slim. All he needed to do, so he would think, was keep us talking till the cavalry arrived.

'Respect,' I said. 'Respect for Bull here, for Red, for Jerome at the hotel, for Jackson. For anyone who is not a white Anglo Saxon protestant.'

O'Hara laughed.

The door opened and Slim walked in. Bull had his gun out and pressed against the back of Slim's head before he knew what was happening. The confident look on O'Hara's face evaporated.

'Don't move a muscle,' Bull said to Slim. 'I

have very itchy fingers.'

'You can't do this,' O'Hara said incredulously. 'You can't just walk in here and pull a gun.'

'Two guns,' I said, taking mine from the back of the waistband of my jeans.

'Make that three,' Red said.

I moved closer to O'Hara and looked down at him.

'Listen,' I said. 'Listen well. My friends and I think you're some kind of dinosaur living in a world beyond its time. We think you're the biggest bigot we've ever seen. And we're going to tell the world about it. How do you think that is going to help your campaign for the presidency?'

'You say one word and I'll sue you for every penny you have.'

'And how are you going to do that?' Bull said.

'My lawyers will find a way.'

'And who might they be?' I said.

'The best in the state — Crane, Oaks and Crane.'

I put the gun back in my waistband and turned to Bull. I nodded at him and he lowered his gun.

'Thanks, Senator,' I said as we walked out. 'That's all I need to know.'

'Well, zip-a-dee-doo-dah,' added Bull.

14

It was hard, punishing work. Constantly bending down to push the wheelbarrows meant that our backs felt it the most, closely followed by our biceps from the lifting of the handles. I'm sure we all felt fitter as the days went by. One of the happier consequences was seeing Pieter regain his shape. He'd lost a lot of weight and his stomach was flat again; across his body, excess fat was turning back to muscle. He seemed to grow mentally as well, pride in his appearance returning; he felt, I was sure, that he could hold his own amongst us now.

However, what wasn't so good was that it was all taking far too long. If it hadn't been for the raid on the bikers' camp, we wouldn't have stood a chance of finishing it before they attacked. Defenceless, no matter how confident we purported to be, they would have swarmed all over us. The raid had bought us valuable time and we were using it well.

Stan and I dumped our loads from the wheelbarrows and stood up to stretch our backs.

'Let's take a breather,' I said, picking up

two bottles of water and passing one to him. 'Tell me about your hotel.'

'It's a fine place,' he said, his chest swelling with pride. 'Right size, too. Just fifteen bedrooms; any more and the service wouldn't be as personal, any less and it would hard to make a profit. Restaurant seats forty, although we need to boost the numbers to fill it.'

'Reputations take a while to build,' I said.

'And an instant to lose.' He wiped the sweat off his body with the T-shirt that he had taken off at the start of the morning's shift. 'Still, I know what you mean. Been going less than a couple of months. Can't expect miracles.'

'But I bet you ask for them from your staff.'

'Always give of your best,' he said. 'No other way in life. Not if you want to hold your head high.'

'You said it was by a lake,' I said. 'Why go for that rather than the sea? Poland does have a coast, doesn't it?'

'The coast is too far north — weather's too cold for much of the year, too seasonal. Lake's much warmer. Did you know Poland has the highest number of lakes of any country in the world?'

'So not just famous for its dill pickles?'

He looked me in the eye. 'You're ribbing me,' he said. 'But I don't mind — that's your way and I'm used to it. No shame in feeling pride in your country, no matter where you come from.'

'What's the lake like?' I asked.

'The hotel is on the shores of Lake Solina in the southeast of Poland. The climate's good and it's a favourite spot for tourists — Poles mainly, since not many people outside the country know enough about the lake or the country as a whole. One day they'll learn and probably force the locals out. Till then it's a fine place to live. Come visit. Bring Anna. I'll give you the best room in the hotel.'

'We'd expect nothing less, but would be happy to settle for whatever you gave us. Wouldn't want to turf out a deserving paying guest.'

'No one more deserving than you,' he said. 'If it hadn't been for you and the money you shared among us in Amsterdam, then I'd never been able to afford the hotel. I can't thank you enough.'

'It wasn't giving — you earned it. I'm grateful for what you all did. Good to have friends you can count on.'

He nodded. 'Reckon so,' he said.

There was a silence between us for a while.

We were both comfortable with it — didn't need always to be talking. Sometimes silence speaks volumes.

'Ho's a good kid,' I said. 'How old do you think she is — twenty?'

'She's twenty-five — small for her age, but I suppose many Chinese are. Her cooking may need a few tweaks — '

'Few tweaks!'

'OK, back to basics is probably more accurate, but boy, can she fight! Did you see her in that ruckus at the bar? She held her own there. Didn't need any help. Not till that guy pulled that gun. Good that you were able to react so quickly. If you hadn't, at least one of us would be dead by now.'

'You're kind of fond of Ho, aren't you?'

He blushed. 'Not in that sense,' he said quickly. 'More like a daughter.' He let out a breath — about as much emotion as you could get from Stan. 'Don't have any family — no wife, no kids. I expect that it's a common situation in our profession. Don't want any ties — no one to cry over your grave when the day comes when you meet the man who's better than you.' He took a long swig from the bottle of water. 'I'm getting a bad feeling about this man in black. He could be the one — the one who's quicker on the draw or a better shot.'

'Time will tell. I have a feeling that he's not going to give up — that death is the only thing that will stop him. His death or ours.'

'Maybe I shouldn't get too attached to Ho. Or she to me. Hate for it to turn out badly.'

'You can't go through life like that. Mustn't suppress your feelings in case something goes wrong. Men like us should treat every day as if it could be our last. Live for the moment. Grab whatever love you can when it comes around. Funny, but until Anna came along I probably felt the same way as you. Now I wouldn't be without her for the world. If it all ends tomorrow, it will be at the happiest time of my life. Before Anna, I didn't belong — except as a part of you guys. Anna made me realize that wasn't enough.'

He looked away. Cast a glance at the ranch house. He gulped.

'Hell,' he said. 'Can't spend all day stretching our backs. There's a pit to dig.'

'And a big one, too,' I said.

'Reckon so,' he said.

* * *

At the end of the day I showered and changed. I reckoned one more day and the pit would be finished. After that it would be the easier tasks of fixing the stinger, the trip wires and the rest of our defences. I put my gun in the shoulder holster, slipped a lightweight jacket over the top and headed into the town.

Jerome was in his usual spot, dog by his side. As I approached he looked at me and said, 'OK, I'll do it. Do it for free this time, too, seeing as you're such a good customer.'

'Do what?'

'You didn't come into town just for your health. You want me to visit my sister again. See what action's going down. What the bikers' plans are now. And, just as important, how many of them are still left.'

'You're wise beyond your years, old man.'

'Be difficult,' he said. 'Well?'

'Well what?'

'Don't I even qualify for a beer?'

I laughed and made for the door.

'And don't forget the peanuts,' he shouted at me.

I came back outside, passed him a beer and flicked a nut at the dog. Caught it OK, but seemed a bit slower today. Maybe the heat was finally getting to it. I took the steak, chopped up small, out of the plastic bag and spread it out on the floor for the dog. He started chomping immediately.

'You keep your word,' Jerome said.

'Only way to be.'

Jerome took a sip of his beer. Sat there deep in thought.

'Are you ready for them if they come right now?' Jerome asked.

I shook my head. 'Need a couple more days, then our work will be complete.'

'Got some surprises up your sleeves?'

'Plenty. And they all depend on them being less smart than your dog.'

'Don't let the dog hear you say that. Might get offended.'

'And we wouldn't want that.'

'No siree. Those gums are lethal weapons.'

He reached down and patted the dog's head. The dog looked up at him and panted, lowered his head and then rolled over. I bent down and tickled his tummy. The dog put all four paws in the air.

'Dog's gonna miss you when you go,' Jerome said. 'I better try to keep you alive as long as possible. Come back tomorrow. If it's more urgent than that, I'll phone you.'

'In that case I hope I don't hear from you.'

'If you're pleased, maybe you could buy me a bourbon. I ain't used to all this beer.'

'If it's good news I'll buy you a bottle.'

'And if it's bad?'

'I'll still buy you a bottle. Won't be your fault.'

He considered this and looked up at me.

'Not just the dog who'll miss you,' he said.

'Feeling's mutual,' I said.

'Now get out before I get sentimental. You'll be giving me a bad reputation.'

'I'll drink to that,' I said, finishing the beer. 'See you tomorrow.'

'God willing,' he said.

'Amen to that.'

15

I couldn't stay away, waiting for a phone call, not knowing the outcome of Jerome's visit to the diner. I went into town and walked down the street to the hotel. Neither Jerome nor his dog was outside. I went inside and asked the helpful receptionist where he was. Out walking the dog, apparently. I found out what was his usual route and started walking. They couldn't have got far — dog didn't look like he had much walking in him.

Jerome was sitting on a roundabout in a children's playground, faithful dog at his feet. I walked over and sat next to him. He was staring out into the distance.

'Sometimes it does you good to go back to your childhood,' he said. 'Look back on your life. See what you did right and what you did wrong. Where you might have been if the dice had rolled a different number.'

'No harm in that,' I said. 'As long as you realize that you can't turn the clock back and take a different path. The die is cast and we have to live what fate sends us.'

'I was one of seven children,' he said. 'Poor family living in a shanty town. Scratching a living where you could. Ma cleaned for the rich folks, took in washing, anything to get a dime. She loved us kids, but we were a burden. As soon as I was old enough I signed up for the army, full ten-year stretch. Army fed me, army clothed me, and I had a little left over from my pay packet to send home to help Ma. Life was good. Had a stint in Korea and managed to come out of that alive.'

'Then what happened?'

'Along came Nam.'

'Ah,' I said.

'Yeah. Ah. I was shipped out along with a lot of kids who were five years my junior. Didn't have any experience of life, straight out of college most of them. Army did the best it could to train them in the time it had, but they were as green as the grass in springtime. Never stood a chance.' He dug in his pocket and picked out half a cheroot, lit it and blew a stream of smoke into the air. 'You should have seen some of the things I saw.'

'I can guess,' I said. 'When we were in the old Yugoslavia — Bosnia, Serbia and the rest — we saw what the Serbs did to their male prisoners. Cut off their genitals and stuffed them in their mouths. Left them to bleed to death. So we signed up with the Muslims to even up the fight. Thought we'd found a just cause. Until we saw what the Muslims did to their prisoners.'

'Cut off their genitals and stuffed them in their mouths?' he said. 'Left them to bleed to death?'

I nodded my head. Then shook it sadly. It was a picture I still saw in my nightmares in all its blood-red vividness.

'It wasn't a fair fight,' he said. 'Yes, we had the equipment and the advantage of numbers. But we were up against guerrilla fighters. Strike, run, hide, strike again and so on. We were butchered. I made up my mind early on that I wouldn't get to know the new recruits — better not to get involved. Less pain that way.'

The dog, as if sensing his need, raised his head and nuzzled into Jerome's feet.

'We used napalm. Never should have been allowed. What you educated people would call indiscriminate. Men, women, children — a mass of flames, screaming as they ran around and burnt to death. I shot some of them to put them out of their misery.' He drew again on the cheroot and was quiet for a while. 'We lost a lot of men — a lot of kids — during that war. And for what? Didn't make no difference to us what happened in Nam. Wasn't going to affect life in the States. Senseless.'

'What happened to you, old man?'

'Purple heart,' he said. 'Shot in the back. Lucky it didn't tear my spine apart.'

'What did you do then?'

'Bummed around. Took whatever work I could — army hadn't trained me for anything useful. Not many jobs going where they need people who can kill. 'Cept your line of business, I suppose.'

'Reckon so,' I said.

'Got a job on the railroad. Maintenance. Working along the track hammering everything so that the rails were tight and there were no gaps. Did that for a long while until I couldn't swing the hammer any more. Pensioned off. Now I carry bags, smile at the visitors and act as the token black. Gives the hotel character, the boss says.'

'Nothing wrong with that,' I said. 'Can still feel some pride in what you do.'

'Sister says it keeps me out of mischief.' He smiled. 'Although what mischief an old man like me is going to get into, I don't know.'

'You're a good man, Jerome. Nothing you could have done for those you lost in Vietnam. Nothing on your conscience.'

'I killed some of the enemy,' he said.

'Sometimes that's what you have to do — them or us. Survive or die.'

'I didn't like doing that.'

'Very few people do. It's only guys like the man in black who can kill without feeling anything. That's what makes him such a formidable foe. He won't hesitate to kill — you don't get any warning.'

'I hope you get him, Johnny. If I were younger, I'd give you a hand. Shooting's like riding a bike — you don't lose that skill. Ain't that right?'

'Yeah. But your reactions slow with age and without constant practice. Some day they're too slow to get you out of trouble. And then the man in black — or someone like him — wins. Once this here is over, it's time for us all to retire again. Hang up our gunbelts and look to a peaceful future.'

'Amen to that,' he said.

'Got some business for you,' I said. 'How busy is the hotel?'

'Wrong time of year for trade — too hot. Got maybe eight or nine rooms free.'

'I want to take all of them.'

'Getting rid of the cannon fodder?'

'I need somewhere for the ranch hands to go when the battle starts. Don't know yet when they will be arriving, but keep the rooms free.'

'News from the diner ain't good. The bikers are still recruiting reinforcements. They're gonna hit you hard. Thirty or so at the moment — they lost a few after your raid. Only the dedicated or the stupid remain. Don't know what the final figure will be, but the odds are gonna be way against you.'

'They won't know what hit them.'

'I'd like to think so,' he said gravely.

'Me too,' I said.

16

The next day passed by uneventfully. We spent time catching up on our sleep, cleaning our guns and filling ourselves with Ho's vastly improving cuisine. All our traps were set and we were ready for the bikers.

Ho came out of the kitchen and put some plates on the table in readiness for dinner.

'How did you come to be here?' I asked. 'Seems a strange place for a young girl to be.'

'I come to America with my parents from Shanghai. We thought it was the land of opportunity. That we could all get better jobs than at home. Shanghai has a lot of poverty, few jobs, even for those willing to do anything. We thought we would have more money and a better lifestyle. We didn't realize how hard it would be for a Chinese person to get a job. We came to Texas because of the oil. Thought there would be plenty of jobs.'

'Oil's mostly mechanized now. Not like in the old days. Not much manual labour around. So what did you do?'

'Mother and Father got work in Chinese laundry — not much pay, hard work, but better than no work at all. I get job as washing up lady in Chinese restaurant. Watch what the cook does. Learn how to cook things. Then the job here comes up. No one seems to want it, but no one will say why not. I come here and cook Chinese meal for Red and he like it. Offers me the job.'

'And then the men start grumbling, I suppose. Chinese food each night loses its charm.'

'I didn't know how to cook American food until Stan comes here. He good teacher. He good man.'

I nodded. 'You know what Stan and the rest of us do?'

'You fight bad men. Rob the rich to pay the poor, like Robin Hood. Protect the weak against the strong.'

'And you know how we do that?'

'You kill bad men. They deserve to die. No problem.'

'It isn't quite that simple, quite that black and white.'

'Doesn't matter. It is result that counts. You bring justice to people who need it. Don't need to know any more.'

'And how did you learn kung fu?'

'Father teach me. Say it will protect from bullies at school. He was right. No one gives me trouble.'

'I'm sorry that you have got caught up in

this. Things will be back to normal soon. The big fight is coming. The last battle. When we win that, everyone can go back to doing their usual jobs with no fear of what will happen to them.'

'I will pray for you.'

'I'd appreciate that.'

Can't do any harm. If there's a god up there, then he's just as likely to speak Chinese as any other language. We need him to smile on us when we go into battle. Surely he'd approve of what we were doing. Agree that to right a wrong sometimes people get hurt. We'd do our best to keep the number down. Can't say fairer than that. Be good to have him on our side. Even up the numbers a little. That's what we needed — a fair fight. And may the best men win.

* * *

Bull pushed his dinner plate away, meal only half-eaten — too painful to chew, I guessed — and got up from the table. He went to where we kept our guns, slung the Kalashnikov over his shoulder and tucked his handgun in the back of his trousers.

'Where are you going?' I asked.

'I'm not sitting around marking time any longer. I'm a patient man,' — *normally, yes, but not with toothache* — 'and I'm not going to sit here waiting for the inevitable. Every day that goes by, they get stronger and our nerves jangle a bit more. I'm going to issue a challenge. Get this thing over and done with.'

'And you're going to go alone?' Red said.

'If I have to,' Bull replied.

'Hell,' I sighed. 'Let's tool up. Can't have you going into the lion's den without any back-up.'

'Just as long as you know this is my show. OK?'

'I'll take that as gratitude for us coming along, shall I?'

'Take it however you like. One way or another, this has got to be done, and done now.'

'What's the plan?' Stan asked. 'We can't go without a plan.'

'I'm going to shout at them a lot,' Bull said.

'Can't beat a simple plan,' I said.

Stan looked horrified. 'I need time,' he said. 'We need to know what we're going to do when we get to the diner. Who's going to be on point, who'll take the flanks, who'll mind the back door.'

'Work it out while we're driving there,' Bull said. 'As long as I get to do the shouting — and the shooting, if it comes to that.'

We went to the back of the room and got

ourselves ready. I slipped on the shoulder holster over my T-shirt, slotted the Browning inside so that it was in full view and picked up the Uzi. I put in a spare clip of bullets for the gun in the right-hand pocket of my jeans, walked back to the table to take a sip of water: mouth dry, hands sweat, that's how it starts.

'Give me a minute,' I said.

I went out of the door and over to the bunkhouse. The ranch hands looked at me and the Uzi in my hand. 'It's time to leave,' I said. 'Rooms are ready for you at the hotel. I'll send Ho out to you and then you get out of here. We'll let you know when it's safe to come back.'

They started getting their things together. It didn't take long. Drifters don't have many possessions.

'This is it?' the grizzled old man said.

I nodded.

'Good luck, mister,' he said.

'Thanks,' I said. 'I hope we meet again in better circumstances. Although if we meet again any circumstances will be good.'

I walked out of the bunkhouse and back to where the four of them were assembled.

'Get Ho,' I said to Stan. 'She goes to town, too. We can look after ourselves for a while.'

'If we survive,' said Pieter.

'I'll die of boredom otherwise,' said Bull.

Stan went into the kitchen and came back with Ho. She went to her room, grabbed some clothes and a washbag and went back to stand with Stan. He took her by the shoulders, bent down and kissed her on the forehead. Turned her around and pointed her to the door. 'Till we meet again,' he said.

She turned to me. 'Look after him for me. He means a lot to me.'

'I'll do my best to keep him safe,' I said. 'He means a lot to us, too.'

She walked out of the door; soon after, I heard the sound of engines kicking into life. The sound faded as they moved into the distance.

'OK,' I said. 'Let's go.'

We squeezed into the jeep and set off.

Five minutes into the drive, Stan spoke.

'It's Bull's show,' he said. 'He takes point. Johnny, you and Red take the flanks. Pieter watches the back door and I stand in front of him ready to reinforce whatever area they attack. We use the assault rifles first and save the handguns for a last resort. If they're spread out, we get them into a tight bunch so that we limit their freedom of action and maximize ours. Not much of a plan, but it will have to do.'

'Agreed,' I said. 'If we have to, we shoot to

kill this time. But make sure one of them shoots first so we can claim self-defence.'

Ten minutes later Red slewed the jeep to a halt and swung it around, ready for a fast getaway. We got out and went into our formation.

Some of the bikers were outside the diner doing something to their bikes: repairing the damage we had done previously maybe. The rest were spread out in the camp, lying around. Some of them were smoking and I hoped that it was weed and would slow down their reflexes.

Bull walked forwards. The bikers looked up at him and made some sort of assessment of his demeanour, not to mention the Kalashnikov. I was hoping for fear, but would settle for bewilderment.

'Bring me the Fixer,' Bull shouted.

I walked over to the diner and waved the Uzi at the bikers who were there and herded them into the main part of the camp. Red and his trusty shotgun was doing the same on the right. Some were behind us and Pieter waved his gun, pointing at the rough circle that had been formed. Pretty soon we had them all in that circle.

The grey-haired man from the bar walked forward to stand in front of Bull. The heavily built Mansion stood by his side, fists clenched and ready for action.

'What are you doing here?' Fixer asked.

'Come to look into the eyes of a coward,' Bull said.

'Who you calling a coward?' Fixer said.

'How many men do you need to take on us five? Thirty, Fifty? Whatever you settle on won't be enough. You might as well hit us now and get it over with.'

'Hit you while you've got the weapons and we're defenceless. What do you think we are? Stupid?'

'Reckon so,' Bull said. 'Stupid cowards, then.'

I could see Fixer tense up, his shoulders raised and his arms stiffened.

'I've come to give you life or death,' Bull said. 'Either way it don't make any difference to me. Your choice.'

'I choose life,' Fixer said.

'Then get on your bikes and ride on,' said Bull.

'Can't do that,' Fixer said. 'We took a contract and have to fulfil it to get our money. Won't look good if we back down.'

'Then you've chosen death,' Bull said. 'So be it.'

The Fixer looked at him and stood there wondering. Couldn't make out Bull or his words.

'You come to us tomorrow morning,' Bull said. 'The time is up to you, but we'll be waiting, Waiting to give you death. If you don't come, we'll come back here and give you death. There's no way out for you now. You have made your choice.'

Bull backed away and the rest of us followed suit, keeping our rifles pointing at the circle of bikers until we were back at the jeep. We climbed in and Red sped away.

'Happy now?' I said to Bull.

'Be happier when it's all over,' he said.

'Seems like it won't be long now.'

'Reckon so,' he said.

'Life or death,' I said. 'And they chose death. How stupid can a person be? We've shown them what we can do and they still choose to face us.'

'Discretion is the better part of valour,' Pieter said.

'You make it sound noble,' I said. 'There's nothing noble about outnumbering your enemy ten to one.'

'Won't be a fair fight,' Bull said. 'Because they still don't know us.'

'Won't get much sleep tonight,' I said.

'Haven't had much sleep for a while now. Good to get it over and done with.'

'As long as the result is right.'

'There's always that,' said Bull. 'Not worth

thinking about the opposite. Can't do nothing about that.'

'When we get back,' said Stan, 'we clean the guns and go over the plan. Sleep in shifts, two hours at a time. Up before dawn and ready to go. Take up our firing positions. Any questions?'

There was no answer. Life or death. Tomorrow fate would show what it had in store for us.

17

They weren't early risers. They hit us a couple of hours after dawn. We were ready for them. As per the plan, we were at the forward firing-points, armed with our handguns and assault rifles. They were going to have to use their brains to get past us, so we thought we had the advantage there. There were fewer than we had expected, but more than we had hoped. At a rough count, I reckoned there were about thirty.

Pieter and I were to the left of our defensive positions, Bull and Stan to the right and Red facing front with his shotgun. They came riding in a column, three abreast, which was pretty stupid — easy target. After all we had done: the fight in the bar, facing down the man in black, the attack on their camp, they still underestimated us. The lead riders dismounted to kick aside our flimsy barrier and, unsuspecting, rode down the middle of the track straight towards the pit.

If I hadn't been so tense I would have laughed. It was like a magic trick. One moment the lead bikes were there, the next they had disappeared. The second row of the column was too close to the first, so had no time to react: they followed into the pit. That was six bikers who, if they weren't injured, now had to fight on foot — if they had the guts for it. We laid down fire on both flanks to keep them moving. The rest of the column swerved round the pit and, contained by our hail of bullets, formed back into the column and headed towards the barbed wire of the stinger.

It was the same story. The front row of the column was into the stinger before the row behind could react. The tyres didn't immediately deflate, but psychologically it was another round to us.

Before they knew it, the re-formed column was approaching the oil. We continued to spray the flanks of the column with bullets, aiming at tyres and legs. They were sitting ducks. Bikes skidded on the oil, dislodging their riders. Those we had hit in the legs limped away back to where they had come from or just lay there groaning and immobile. The numbers were decreasing at last.

The trip wires accounted for another three bikers, throwing them off their bikes and sending them backwards through the air. Half the original force was now on foot. From here on it would be fire power and accuracy that would decide the result of the battle. Our job at the front of the defences now done, we retreated to the next line of firing positions. We would fire, move, fire, creating the impression of larger numbers on our side and, at the same time, making us less of a target.

The grey-haired man, his long ponytail hanging down from his helmet, was still on his bike, Mansion at his side. The Fixer tried to marshal his troops, waving his arms to get them to form two wings that could encircle us. While he was doing this, we kept on firing. The bikers didn't know where to turn, every move presented danger. Some had had enough; they turned their bikes around and headed home.

I used the Browning to fire more accurately and hit a couple of bikers in the thighs before moving to the next position. Behind me I heard the boom of Red's shotgun and saw two men blown off their bikes by its force.

Those remaining had drawn handguns and were starting to return fire, a fruitless exercise for those on bikes since their movement reduced their chance of hitting us to close to zero. We fell back to the final level of firing positions outside the ranch house. There was the sound of shooting all around and it became increasingly difficult to work out exactly what was going on — there are times when you smell the battle and hear the battle, but don't see it, as things are happening too fast. Each of us had to concentrate on our own targets. I was coming close to having to reload the Browning, so switched back to the Uzi until I got the opportunity. Behind me, I heard Stan cry out. He was hit.

I turned round and indicated that he and Pieter should head for the ranch house. Stan was clutching his shoulder as he ran back.

The only cover for the bikers was the defensive positions we had just vacated, but staying there wouldn't do them any good. How could they progress when we were pinning them down? The grey-haired man shouted something I couldn't hear against the cracks of the handguns, the volleys from the assault rifles and the deafening boom of the shotgun. Four of the bikers broke cover and tried rushing us. We cut them down before they had taken half a dozen paces.

It was the trickiest period now. Those bikers who were still mobile were beginning to get to our two flanks, those on foot were trying to advance directly towards us. We were constantly having to watch two threats at once. I would shoot at a target straight ahead and then swivel round to aim to my side. It was time for the next phase of our plan.

I shouted across at Bull and he turned his rifle to the right flank. I did the same on the left. Freed from fire, those who were ahead of us started to run forward. We let them come, all the time picking off the bikers on our flanks. There were men toppling off bikes on both sides, the numbers being whittled down with each of our bursts of fire.

The men on foot rushed forward. Bull and I turned and ran in an arc. We were now behind them. Red was in front of them and Pieter and Stan were at their posts at the windows of the ranch house. Instead of them surrounding us, we had them caught on all sides.

The Uzi gave the chilling click that told me it was time to reload. Through years of practice I didn't have to look at the gun while I pulled out the spent magazine and clicked in a full one. There were bodies going down like pins in a bowling alley. Red fired his shotgun again and two of the men on bikes tumbled to the ground, their bodies trapped underneath their bikes.

I fired a shot at the Fixer and caught him in the shoulder. He spun round with the impact and I then shot him in the back — ignoble, maybe, but effective. Seeing their leader fall took the spirit out of the rest of them. Hands went up in the air. Pieter and Stan emerged from the ranch house and started to round up the bikers into a group. I looked across at Bull; he and Mansion were having a face-off, both standing up with a gun aimed at the other.

'Looks like an impasse,' I called out. 'You can kill each other or we can work something out. Remember Bosnia, Bull? When the battle was going nowhere?'

Bull nodded and looked at Mansion.

'Let's see who's the better man between us two,' Bull said to Mansion. 'Wrestle me, bare hands. If you win you go free. If I win, you give yourself up. How does that sound?'

The cogs in Mansion's brain whirred for a while. 'You got a deal,' he said. 'I know who's the better man. You ain't got a chance.'

'OK,' Bull said. 'Throw your gun to the side and face me.'

Mansion threw his gun twenty feet to his side.

Bull smiled.

'Sucker,' he said, pointing his gun at Mansion's head. 'Put your hands up and move to where the rest of your friends are.'

'But that's not fair,' Mansion said. 'We had a deal.'

'And I've just reneged on it,' said Bull. 'Get moving.'

We rounded them up and assessed the damage. Stan had blood coming from a wound in his left arm and Pieter was limping — there was a dark stain spreading along his thigh. Bull and I were unhurt. Not too bad considering the odds we had faced. I took my phone out and called the sheriff.

'Safe to come now,' I said. 'It's all over.'

* * *

Tucker took one look at the scene, then called for reinforcements from the state cops and a fleet of ambulances.

'Well, boys,' he said while we were waiting. 'Looks like you've been having a real humdinger of a party here. Your guests don't seem to have enjoyed it much, though.'

'Didn't seem to like our mercenary hospitality,' I said. 'Can't please all of the people all of the time.'

'In your case some of the people some of the time would be an improvement.' He looked at me seriously. 'Is this the end of it?'

'I hope so, Sheriff. Not much more they can throw at us.'

'What about the man in black? He doesn't seem to be among the bodies round here.'

I shook my head. 'He works alone — hard to catch a man when he works alone. He's a professional, but he messed up badly in thinking he could rely on a bunch of bikers to defeat us. I'd like to think his contract is now terminated.'

'And who do you think hired him?'

'I'm pretty certain it's the senator, but I don't have any hard evidence.'

'Pretty certain won't be enough for me to hold the senator on any charge.'

'Maybe if we catch the man in black he might give us a name. Make a statement to save his own skin.'

'And the chances of that?'

'Not good,' I said. 'Maybe you could circulate his description. The state cops could cast a wider net.'

'State cops aren't your best friends. Do you realize how much paperwork will have to be filled in as a result of this?' He waved his arm in an arc that encompassed the large group of bikers being guarded by Bull and Red. 'Hell, I don't know if they'll even have enough tape to record all the interviews.'

'I should have thought of that when we were facing thirty bikers. Mustn't increase the paperwork. How stupid of me.'

'Foolhardy, maybe, but not stupid,' he said. 'Those mean streets will be a little less mean from now on.' He gave me a look I hadn't seen him use before. 'Shake my hand, Mr Actually. You did well. Though I hate to admit it, mind.'

He thrust his hand towards me and I shook it. Somewhere beneath that hard exterior I thought I detected a subtle difference — a softness, sentimentality even, that he probably didn't allow out much on its own. 'So whatever you did,' he said, 'don't do it again.'

'No, Sheriff,' I said.

'Not unless you have to, that is,' he said, giving me a wink.

The ambulances arrived first, but I guess that was best. There was no rush for the demoralized and bloody crew that now sat on the grass in front of the ranch house. The state cops were the second priority.

The good news was that Stan and Pieter's injuries were minor. Both bullets had passed right through, leaving large exit wounds. They were going to need a lot of patching up, but they'd survive to fight another day — if necessary.

The state cops arrived in force. There were three motorcycle policemen in leathers and white helmets, four squad cars with every seat occupied and a van full of cops with weapons at the ready. Tucker helped their man in charge to do a kind of triage on the bikers — those going to hospital, who needed guards, those who were in no state to cause any threat and could go with just the paramedics, and those who would go straight to jail.

As everybody was ferried away from the ranch, the adrenaline started to wear off. I needed a strong black coffee and a shot of something, anything, as long as it was alcohol, the stronger the better. The remaining three of us walked into the ranch house, put our weapons on the table and then headed straight to the bar that Stan had set up. I poured a slug of bourbon while I decided what I was going to drink. It didn't hit the sides, just slid down real easy. I looked at my watch. It was still only eight in the morning. I reckoned that the whole battle had only taken maybe twenty minutes, but, as always, it had seemed like a lifetime.

Bull arrived with a pot of coffee and three mugs. 'Do you think we should tell the guys in the bunkhouse that it is safe to come out?' he said.

'Give me a moment,' said Red, pouring a shot of Jack Daniels. I noticed his hand was shaking. 'Hell,' he said. 'I must be out of practice. Never used to shake.'

'Yes, you did,' I said. 'We all did, but only when it was over. Memory plays tricks with us, that's all.'

Bull turned to me. 'Thanks for the reminder of Bosnia.' He gave out a deep laugh. 'They fall for it every time.' He shook his head disbelievingly. 'Still, nice to be trusted, even if it is by those who don't have a brain cell.'

There was a knock on the door and a tall man in an immaculate grey suit came in. He had dark hair receding at the temples and flecked with grey at the sides. His face was weather-beaten and world-weary. He looked like he had seen it all before: nothing new under this relentless sun.

'Which one of you is Johnny Silver?' he said.

'That would be me.'

'I'm Captain Rogers, State Police,' he said. 'I think you've got a story to tell me. And, before you start, Tucker has told me all about you. Cut the wise guy, OK?'

I nodded. Didn't seem there was much to say. I couldn't deny it.

'Let's go back a few nights. You wouldn't happen to know anything about an attack on a diner.'

'What diner?'

'Thought so,' he said. 'Now let's fast forward to this morning. What's your story?'

'We were quietly sipping coffee, enjoying the sweet morning air that you get in these parts, when all of a sudden these bikers turn up waving pistols. We couldn't sit there and do nothing about it, so we used reasonable force to defend our property.'

'Reasonable force? Do you call Kalashnikovs reasonable force?'

'And an Uzi,' I said.

'What did I say?'

'Sorry, it's a hard habit to break. Forget the bit about the Uzi. What would you do in those circumstances?'

'Call in a SWAT team. But you seem to have one of those already, don't you?

I shrugged.

'These guys show up out of the blue and just happen to fall into a pit you'd dug. And into some barbed wire, and, well you get the picture. Seems a bit coincidental, don't you think?'

'We'd had a run-in with some of the bikers in town last week. They said they'd come back and exact revenge.'

'Exact revenge? Got that wrong, didn't they. I've not seen this kind of carnage for a long while, and that was in Vietnam. I'm surprised you didn't add napalm to your box of tricks.'

'We knew we would be heavily outnumbered, so we had to try to even up the odds a little. What else could we do? Call on you and expect you to mount an around-the-clock guard team?'

'Point taken,' he said. 'But we can't let a bunch of vigilantes run the county.'

'Don't seem like a good job has been done in the past. Did Tucker tell you about our ranch hand who was beaten to a pulp? Not to mention all the other incidents that have been going down?'

'Tucker mentioned something of the sort. You got any unfinished business?'

'There's the man in black. He's still out there somewhere.'

'Tucker told me about him. Is he behind all this?'

'He set up today's battle. But someone's pulling his strings.'

'Any ideas?'

'I've not got any proof, but I think it's Senator O'Hara.'

'Boy, this day just keeps getting better and better. The last thing I need is the senator on my back. What's behind all this?'

'It all leads back to land. Someone wants it and is prepared to play dirty to get it.'

'Haven't had a range war here since the days of the Wild West. Seems to me you guys would have fitted in there real fine.'

'We each do what we're good at. It's our business to defend the weak and right wrongs.'

'Laudable. But someone has to clean up the mess you leave. And that someone happens to be me. I'm the one who has to work out how to get six motor bikes out of a pit nine feet deep.' He sighed.

'We could just bury them,' I said. 'We've got all the soil we took out.'

'Unfortunately, there's six men stuck in the hole as well.'

'Would anyone miss them?'

'Probably not, but I happen to like my job and don't want to get busted and finish up back on the beat.' He looked at me and shook his head. 'I pity the sheriff. Go see Tucker later today and give him full statements. And then don't go anywhere. I might want to talk to you again, although I sincerely hope not.'

He nodded his head at me, roved his gaze over the others, then turned his back and walked away.

18

My mobile rang. It sounded deafening. Then I realized that it wasn't the mobile, it was me. Somewhere inside my head a pixie was using a sledge-hammer to wake me up. I instantly regretted all the celebration we had done last night and all the booze that had gone with it. I fumbled around, felt the phone and sat upright on the bed. I looked at my watch — it said ten o'clock. Even the lie-in hadn't done me any good.

I answered the call. It was Jerome, sounding agitated, a strange hollowness in his voice.

'You better come to town straight away,' he said. 'Something bad has happened. I got to go. I'll explain when I see you.'

'What's up?' Bull asked.

I started to get dressed. 'Jerome. Says something bad has happened. I'm going to town.'

'Sounds like I should come with you. Watch your back. Another pair of hands. Whatever.'

'Curiosity?'

'Bit of that, too.'

We dressed quickly and woke Red to tell him where we were going. He insisted on coming too and grabbed the keys to the jeep. We jumped in and he sped away across country to avoid the pit. At some stage we would have to fill it in and give Pa Blenkenstein his digger back. Seemed like that could wait.

Red skidded the jeep to a halt outside the hotel, a cloud of dust coming from the wheels. There were two horses tied up to a rail. I recognized them as the ones the girls had ridden. My heart dropped to my boots.

Jerome was standing on the porch with Cameron in his arms. Her shoulders were shaking.

We jumped out of the jeep and Red ran straight to Cameron. She broke off from Jerome and buried herself in Red's body. He held her tightly. She was sobbing, unable to utter a word.

I went up to Jerome. 'What's going on?' I said.

'Come inside where we can talk without being overheard. We don't want the sheriff getting to know what happened.'

We went inside and Jerome led us to a table in an alcove. We were the only people there. Too early even for the hardest drinkers. Bull followed us, then Red and Cameron came in.

We sat down and waited for Jerome to tell us what was wrong. I had a feeling that this would sober us up real good.

'He's got her,' Jerome said. 'I couldn't stop him. He was too strong for an old man like me.'

'Slow down,' I said. 'Who's got who?'

'I don't know his name. Dressed in a black suit. Mirrored aviator sunglasses. Drove up in a silver Mercedes.'

'The man in black,' Bull said. 'Hell! I thought he would have given up; that we'd seen the last of him.'

'He's got Lucy,' Cameron said. 'She didn't have a chance.'

'The two girls were outside,' Jerome said.

'We came to get some shopping,' Cameron added.

'This silver Mercedes pulls up right by them,' Jerome said. 'He — the man in black — got out and put a rag or something over Lucy's mouth. She went all limp. He bundled her into the car. I tried to stop him. Grabbed him by the arms, but he hit me and I fell to the floor. The dog didn't like what he had done and attacked him. He shot the dog.' He looked at me sadly. 'He went and shot the dog. Why'd he do that? Dog wouldn't have done him any harm. Hardly got a tooth in his mouth. You know that, Johnny.'

A tear rolled down his cheek.

'He was a good dog,' I said. 'None finer. We'll do right by him. We'll make the man in black pay for what he's done.'

Jerome nodded. 'Make him pay real good.' He reached inside his jacket, pulled out two envelopes. 'Says when you've signed the letters he'll let Lucy go. He'd be in touch with me. Told me that you shouldn't get the law involved. If you do, he'll kill her. Said she's pretty and he might have some fun with her first. Do you think he means it?'

'I'm afraid so,' I said.

'He's mean enough to do anything,' Bull said.

Jerome passed the envelopes to me. One had Rafael's name on it, the other had Red's. I gave one to Red and opened the one to Rafael.

'It's an agreement to buy the ranch,' Red said.

'Same here,' I said.

'All that work for nothing,' Bull said. 'We been wasting our time. He's going to get what he wants after all. We might as well never have come.'

'It's too soon to give up,' I said. 'He has to make the exchange. We've got to stop him getting away with it. Our first priority must be Lucy. We need to think of a way round this. Get her safe and neutralize the man in black for good.'

'Does neutralize mean what I think it do?' asked Red.

'It do,' I confirmed. 'You guys get back. Take Cameron home. I'll ride Lucy's horse back when I'm finished here. Maybe someone could pick me up from the Retreat in a couple of hours.'

'What are you going to do?' asked Bull.

'I got a dog to bury.'

* * *

Jerome's cabin was a ten-minute walk away. We went slowly so as not to tire him out. All the way he cradled the dog in his arms, his eyes moist.

'There's a place out back,' he said. 'Sort of special place for us. We would sit there in the evening when the hotel had shut for the night. I'd give the dog his meal and we'd sit there together, me with a beer and him munching his food. I'd cut it up real small for him. Best part of the day. The heat gone, nothing to hear but the chirruping of the crickets and the hoot of an owl. Won't be the same without him.'

'Go get a spade, Jerome. And some wood, too. Hammer and nails for a cross.' I took the dog from him and set him on the ground in front of a wrought-iron bench. 'Did he have a name?'

'When I first got him I called him Blue, like in the song.'

'You're a good dog, too,' I said.

'You got it,' he said. 'But people laughed at it; one even sprayed him blue for a joke. Wouldn't wash out, had to shave all the hair off him, so he became just 'the dog'.'

'Nothing wrong with that,' I said. 'A rose by any other name.'

'Don't know about that,' he said, 'but he didn't deserve to die, whatever you called him.'

He placed the dog in front of the bench and went inside his cabin. Came back a couple of minutes later with everything we needed. He passed me the spade and I started digging by the side of the bench where the dog would have lain during the evening. It wasn't hard work, just dispiriting. The soil here was much lighter than at Red's ranch and within fifteen minutes I had a rectangular hole big enough to take the body. Jerome set him down in the hole and stood in silence as I filled in the earth I had removed. I made a cross from two pieces of wood and pushed it into the ground where the dog's head would have been. Stood back and surveyed my handiwork. Sighed.

'Got some bourbon indoors,' Jerome said. 'Take a nip with me?'

I nodded and we moved inside his cabin. It wasn't big, but it was real neat: pots and pans shining, hanging from hooks dangling from the ceiling. A bed, made up, in one corner, a pair of cane chairs in another and a small table and two chairs in a third. Jerome got two tumblers from a cupboard, picked up a bottle of bourbon from the table and sat himself down in one of the cane chairs. I sat in the other and took the bourbon he offered me. It slipped down easily. Hair of the dog.

'What you gonna do about this man in black?' Jerome asked, sipping his drink.

'Kill him,' I said. 'We've given him two opportunities to back off, but he keeps coming back. Seems like killing him is the only way to stop him.'

'I ain't never shot a gun, but if I can help you can count on me.'

'Thanks, Jerome. I'll bear that in mind.'

'What's behind all this? Town was peaceful till Red arrived.'

'I think the senator wants to cleanse the town of a half-breed Comanche. Offends his sensibilities. Spoils his idea of paradise. Willing to do anything to achieve his goal. When money wouldn't solve the problem, he turned to dirty tricks — scaring off the ranch hands, poisoning the water, sending in the bikers, now kidnapping Lucy. Don't seem to be an end to it.'

'You could give in,'

'Seems like we may have to.'

'But it would rankle.'

'A hell of a lot.'

He topped up our glasses. Leaned back in the chair and sighed.

'We'll find a way to beat him. We're not finished yet. If he thinks that, he's read us all wrong.'

'Wouldn't like to be on the wrong side of you. You need an edge. Something that the senator and the man in black are not prepared for. Got any ideas?'

'A germ of one, but I have to think it through. Lucy's safety is paramount. Once we can get over that, we can move to the offensive. I think the man in black may have underestimated us yet again.'

'Bad mistake,' Jerome said.

'You betcha.'

* * *

I rode the horse back slowly, partly for its benefit as it wasn't used to someone of my weight, and partly for my benefit as I wasn't used to riding bareback. It was even more difficult than it looked. After a while I decided that I should curl my legs round its belly and trust in the horse. It took nearly an hour to get back to the Retreat, where I found everyone in a sombre mood. No smiles, no singing in the fields. It was as if life had been put on hold and nobody knew how to cope with it.

Rafael came out to greet me. I climbed down and he gave the horse to a teenage boy, who led it off to the stables.

'Good of you to come,' Rafael said.

'Least I could do,' I said. 'I feel responsible for what has happened. If it hadn't been for me you might have taken the offer to sell and never have got involved in this business.'

'Things happen for a purpose,' he said. 'We might not be able to see it now, but in good time all will be revealed.'

'How's Cameron?' I asked. 'Has she got over the shock of it all?'

'She's still upset and very worried about Lucy. We all are. When can we get her back?'

'We have to wait for the man in black to make his play. He's mean enough to make us sweat.'

I showed him the letter, He read it a couple of times so that he was sure what he was committing himself to.

'Do you want me to sign it now?' he said. 'In case things move quickly.'

'Not yet,' I said. 'Leave it with me for a while. I'm working on a plan.'

'It will need to be a good one. You can't take any risks with Lucy's life.'

'I know. Trust me. I wouldn't put her in jeopardy.'

'Are you getting the sheriff involved?'

'The man in black says not to. Can't risk it. It's down to us and us alone.'

'It's a heavy burden,' he said.

I nodded. Suppressed a sigh. Took out my mobile and called Red to come and pick me up. I shook Rafael's hand and started walking. It would help me think. I hoped Stan, having heard what had happened, was having better luck with coming up with a plan. Mine had too many *ifs* in it. Too many *maybes* as well. I inhaled then let the sigh come out. It didn't help.

* * *

It was after dinner and we were back round the long dining table. Red had the map out again and it was spread out before us. Stan was in planning mode.

'We have to second-guess the man in black,' he said. 'Get into his mind. Choose what site he would pick for the exchange. Guard it from a distance. That's our best chance. Take him out with the sniper rifle.'

'I've made that shot once before,' I said. 'I don't know if I could pull it off a second time. It takes a lot of practice and you have to set the sights for the exact distance away from the target. Until we know the place of the exchange, you can't zero the sights. Get anything wrong and you might hit Lucy. It's very risky.'

'Let's get back to that after we've tried to guess the location of the exchange,' Stan said. 'There might be things about the terrain — the amount of cover and so on — that we can use to our advantage. Cut down the risks.'

'Cutting down might not be enough,' said Bull. 'With the girl's life at stake we should be aiming at eliminating all the risks.'

'Red,' I said. 'You know the terrain. Where would you pick for an exchange?'

'It would need to be somewhere where he could keep us at a distance so that attack by handguns is out. Then he would want some cover while doing the exchange and some route for a quick getaway. Let me think for a moment.'

Pieter, always the first to break when drinks were overdue, got up and went to the side table where all the drinks were set up. He picked up some bottles and placed them on the table. To these he added five highball glasses, a tub of ice and some mixers. He poured himself a whiskey and dry and gestured for the rest of us to help ourselves. I picked up a bottle of vodka, poured a large measure into the glass, added ice and orange juice. Took a sip and started thinking. How to outwit the man in black? He'd know we would try to rescue Lucy and not have to sign the forms. He'd be trying to second-guess us. I shook my head at the complexity of bluff and double bluff.

Red stared at the map and shook his head. 'I'm too new to the area. Much of it is still a mystery to me. We need an old hand. Someone who's been around here a while. I'll get Curly — he's been here the longest. He'll be working in the lower pasture. Give me ten minutes and I'll be back with him.'

True to his word, he arrived back ten minutes later with a grizzled guy who looked about sixty — conservatively. He had on a pair of tattered blue jeans and a check shirt. His face was lined from many years of blinking into the sun. He looked like he hadn't shaved for a week, the stubble standing out against the red of his skin. Curly wasn't an apt description any more — he was as bald as a billiard ball and there was sweat on his head. He took out a pipe and looked at Red, waiting for permission to smoke.

'Go ahead,' Red said.

If he'd known what was to follow he would probably have said no. Curly took a penknife and a pouch of tobacco from his pocket. He dug around in the bowl of the pipe and tipped the charred remains of his last smoke into the ashtray. He inspected the bowl and nodded to himself. Then he took a large fingerful of tobacco and flaked it into the pipe. Next he tamped the tobacco down with the end of the penknife, took out a box of matches, struck one and inhaled deeply. He let out a stream of smoke and looked at the bottles on the table.

'Thirsty work,' he said.

'Help yourself,' I said. Anything to get down to business.

He poured himself two fingers of bourbon, added some ice and took a sip.

Red passed the map across the table and explained about the man in black and what we were looking for. Curly was now part of the team.

'Start with a radius of twenty miles,' I said. 'If the man in black has done his homework, he'll know that Sheriff Tucker won't want to get involved, so he'll choose a site within

Tucker's jurisdiction.'

Curly looked at the map for what seemed like an age. Then he finally spoke.

'There's a few possibilities,' he said. 'The first is the silver mine — '

'A silver mine?' I interrupted.

'Don't get excited. You're not about to become a millionaire. It was played out a hundred years ago. But the entrance and mine shafts are still there. Be hard to shoot him if he's in the entrance.'

'How does he get away?' Bull asked. 'Seems like he has backed himself into a corner.'

'No one knows where the tunnels go,' Curly said. 'Could be another exit.'

'I think we're going about this in the wrong way,' Stan said. 'We're trying to get inside the man in black's mind. What would he be looking for?'

'Somewhere quiet,' Pieter said. 'He won't want to get caught by the police. It would need to be a deserted spot.'

'But not too far away from a main road, so he could make a quick getaway,' Bull said.

'He will want to keep us at a distance,' I said. 'Make it as hard as possible for him to be a target.'

'And as easy as possible for him to target us,' Pieter said.

'You know what he's doing right now?' I

said. 'Bending over a map of the area like we're doing. He doesn't know the land hereabouts. He'll be going through the same selection process. Go on, Curly. I want every possible site that conforms to our criteria — reasonably close, easy to defend, just as easy to attack us, fast getaway.'

Curly took a pencil and drew various circles on the map. There were five in total. Hell, I thought. This was going to take some time, which we probably didn't have. Curly leaned back in his chair and admired his handiwork. 'There you go,' he said. 'These are the only alternatives that fit what you're looking for. It's got to be one of these.'

I topped up Curly's bourbon. 'Thanks, Curly,' I said. 'You've been a great help.'

He finished his drink in one big swallow. 'It's been my pleasure,' he said. 'Mind you, anything that gets me out of the sun is a pleasure. Be seeing you, folks.'

After Curly had left there was a deflated mood in the air, together with the clouds of smoke from Curly's pipe.

'One each,' I said. 'Let's start at dawn.'

'We'd need to borrow a couple of the ranch hands' cars. I don't have enough for one for each of us.'

'I'll talk to them tonight,' Bull said.

'And no one will say no to you.'

'Exactly,' he said.

'Looks like we got the start of a plan,' I said. 'Can I have your letter, Red?'

'What for?' he asked, passing it across the table to me.

'I'm working on a fall-back plan,' I said.

'Are you going to enlighten us?' Pieter said.

Bull grunted. 'You should know him by now.'

'I take that as a no then,' Pieter said.

I nodded. 'Not formed enough yet. Still in the embryonic phase. I don't want to have you laugh at me. Trust me,' I said.

'That one again,' said Bull. 'You usually only say that when someone's gonna start shooting.'

'Maybe it will be different this time,' I said.

'Maybe,' Bull said, shaking his head. 'Maybe.'

19

I headed down a winding country road which was the third side of a triangle bordered by Route 10 and Route 20 and ending at Fort Stockton. My destination was a flat valley in the hills halfway down the road — if you could call it a road. I was driving a beat-up flatbed truck that wouldn't have looked out of place in an old black-and-white movie of the Great Depression, but beggars can't be choosers. We'd only just managed to scrape together sufficient vehicles for the reconnaissance trips. The problem was that damned pit — most of the vehicles owned by the ranch hands couldn't cope with going across country to avoid the pit.

Even with both windows wound down, the inside of the truck was like an oven The black colour of the truck absorbed heat and the wound-down windows merely circulated that heat without cooling it to any degree. I reached across to the passenger seat and picked up a bottle of water, drank a large gulp to help combat the dehydration. I was en route to what had once been a private airstrip used by its owners for flying lessons, but the recession had killed off that market. It stood desolate with a shimmering haze rising up from the weed-ridden runway.

As soon as I saw the place I knew it would be ideal for the man in black's purposes. There was a disused hangar and a small control tower; the rest was open space. Impossible to approach without being seen from a few hundred yards away. Whoever controlled the hangar controlled the airstrip. A rag of a windsock hung limply in the still air as if it had given up hope.

I drove round the perimeter — frustratingly there was only one way in and out — brought the truck to a halt and went across to the hangar. I pulled open the tall corrugated-iron doors and stepped inside. There was the smell of diesel in the still air. There were three oil drums, big enough for a man to hide behind, but the man in black had the advantage of knowing the rendezvous ahead of us and would surely search the area thoroughly. No way could we get one of us inside without being spotted by even the most cursory examination.

There was an inspection pit which vehicles could be driven over for a mechanic to work underneath. But the same applied to it as to the oil drums: anyone in the pit would be easily spotted and neutralized. Dejected, I walked back outside and looked up at the roof. It had a shallow slope where a man could lie in wait and fire down, but you would have to get there well in advance and the man in black wouldn't be giving us any time for preparation, All in all a hopeless situation.

I thought for a moment about splitting our forces — never a good idea — and placing one of us at each of the five probable sites so that we had these covered before we knew the precise rendezvous. But the man in black was a professional. He'd scour each trap for a possible ambush. We might as well stay as a group and hope to outgun him with our firepower, if we could get close enough to get a clear shot at him without putting Lucy at risk. If, pilgrim, if.

I checked out the control tower; there was a good view through the Plexiglas windows. There was a round table in the middle of the control room, maps still on its top. Various routes — flight paths, I supposed — were marked out on the maps. A plastic mug which probably once contained coffee stood on a filing cabinet. It was green and furry. Long time since it had been touched. The big disadvantage of the control tower was that, though you could see for miles, the windows didn't open, so there was no point considering it as an ambush position. As it was

Plexiglas you wouldn't be able to smash it to provide a hole to shoot through.

Reconnaissance over, I got in the truck and sweated my way back to town. I hoped the others were having better luck.

The town was quiet, it still being early, and the majority of shops were not open yet. I approached the hotel and saw Jerome on the porch as usual, except there was no dog lying at his feet. I went inside, spoke to the receptionist, sweet-talked her for a favour and came back out with two strong black coffees. I handed one to Jerome.

'Too early for a beer,' I said.

'Don't seem to have the thirst on me any more.'

He took a sip of the coffee and looked up at me with half-closed eyes and a smile.

'Bourbon,' I said. 'Just enough to get the blood circulating.'

'Purely medicinal,' he said. 'In that case — how do you Limeys say it? — cheers.'

'How do you feel about meeting the man in black again?'

'If I was thirty years younger I would jump at the chance to settle the score. Ain't got the fight in me any more either.'

'Sounds good,' I said. 'Exactly what I'm looking for. You're to be the man in black's go-between. You won't pose any threat to him. Get him to use you in the exchange: the letters for the girl. He won't want any of us getting close, so you'd be the ideal candidate.'

'What do I have to do?'

'I haven't figured that out yet.'

'Just let me know,' he said. 'I'll do whatever I can for the girl, and to get even if we can.'

We finished our coffees in silence, neither of us needing to speak. We knew that each of us could rely on the other. I thought of the coming exchange. Hoped it wouldn't be long now for Lucy's sake. I went inside with the empty mugs and collected the copies of the letter that the receptionist had made for me. I stopped off at the gunsmith to buy six more handguns — you can never have too many guns — and headed back for the ranch, hoping the others had had a more fruitful time.

* * *

They hadn't. Couldn't eliminate any of the five most probable sites. Might have to be the shot from the sniper's rifle after all.

'Sign this,' I said to Red, handing him the letter.

He took it, found a pen and scrawled his name. One for the man in black. All I needed now was Rafael's signature and we would be in a position to give the man in black what he wanted.

'How's your fall-back plan going?' Stan asked.

'Still developing.'

'Will it be ready in time?'

'I hope so. We've not got a good plan A. We need a different approach. All I can do is try to buy us some time so that we can take out the man in black.'

'What preparations should we be making?'

'We'll take two vehicles — the jeep and the flatbed truck. There's a chance that we could put one of us in the back screened out of view by the tailgate. Each of us needs to be fully armed — assault rifles, handguns, one each on show, one each hidden and, for me, the sniper rifle.'

'Still intent on making that shot?' Bull asked.

'Last resort only.'

'Feels like we're at that stage already,' he said.

'Jerome said to me we needed an edge. That's what my fall-back plan is trying to utilize. If it wasn't for Lucy we could simply surround him and wait till he runs out of ammunition, but it's the girl who's the problem. He'll use her as a shield and keep us at bay. Take the girl out of the equation and the odds favour us and not him.'

'And how are you going to do that?' Red asked.

'I'm going to use Jerome.'

'Jerome!' Bull said. 'You're going to pit an old man against the man in black? Hell, Johnny, I've heard some half-baked schemes in the past, but this one takes the gold prize.'

'Got a better idea?'

Silence.

'That settles it then,' I said. 'I'm off to the Retreat to get Rafael's signature. I'll call you if I hear anything. Be prepared to move quickly.'

Bull was still shaking his head and saying, 'Jerome!' as I left.

20

He chose the aerodrome. The call from Jerome came through late afternoon. We were to be at the exchange point just before dusk, giving the man in black another advantage: fading light. He stipulated that all five of us and Jerome should come; that way he could see where we all were and eliminate any chance of an ambush on his way out. If anyone else came, especially the police, then the deal was off and he would kill Lucy. I knew he wasn't bluffing.

I told Jerome we'd pick him up in an hour. We spent the time on displacement activity — cleaning already pristine rifles and handguns, poring over the map that we knew by heart. At six o'clock we set off. I hoped that each of us, including Lucy, would be coming back in one piece.

We picked up Jerome and I ran him through the fall-back plan a second time. I gave him the two letters and a handgun, more for reasons of instilling confidence than anything else. He tucked the letters in a pocket inside his coat and, from the same pocket produced a small bottle of bourbon.

He took a swig to steady his nerves; I would have done the same in his position. No matter how many times you are in these sorts of circumstances, the nerves still jangle. Wouldn't be human otherwise. I speculated as to whether the man in black was feeling the same way now. Doubted it.

The Mercedes was parked just outside the hangar. The engine was running. The man in black got out and stood with the car shielding his lower half. He rested a rifle on the roof.

'Move away from the vehicles,' he shouted. 'Don't stop until I say so.'

We moved to our left. I judged that the distance between us was only a hundred yards. I'd need to adjust for that, if I got the chance. Worse, though, was the fact that we were sitting targets, no cover anywhere.

'We need to split up,' Stan said. 'Cover him from different angles.'

We carried on moving, but at different speeds, so that we were stringing ourselves out.

'Lay your guns down,' he shouted.

'Let's see the girl first,' I shouted back.

He opened the back passenger door of the car and dragged Lucy out. She seemed to stumble, but caught her balance and stood up so we could see her.

'Now lay down your guns,' he said.

We made great play in laying down the assault rifles and then, from shoulder holsters purposely worn for the occasion, our handguns. He didn't know that each of us had a gun in the backs of our waistbands, To find that out he would have to search us and he couldn't risk being that close.

'Send the black guy over here with the letters,' he called out.

'Let the girl start walking,' I called back.

'No dice. She stays here until I have the letters.'

'No can do,' I said. 'Why should I trust you? No, she walks to the middle and stays there. When Jerome verifies that she's OK, then he'll bring the letters to you.'

He thought for a while. 'OK,' he said. 'But no tricks or the girl gets it. Send the old man.'

Jerome started walking. He didn't walk fast at the best of times, but these fifty yards or so seemed to be taking an age. Still, that was good. It meant that Lucy was actually nearer to us than had been intended. Jerome held her at arm's length while he inspected her to make sure nothing bad had happened. He spoke to her, but didn't get an answer.

'She's drugged up,' Jerome called. 'Apart from that, she seems OK.'

'Take him the letters,' I called.

Jerome left Lucy and walked to the man in

black. He handed him the two letters. The man in black saw the signatures and was happy. Jerome, as per the plan, immediately started walking back. When he was level with Lucy, he quickly shoved her to the ground so that she was lying flat, face down. He covered her with his body. That was our signal.

We drew our spare guns and threw ourselves to the ground. All except me; I raced to the pick-up truck and jumped on to the flatbed back. I threw the tailgate down and lay flat with the sniper rifle tucked into my armpit. By this time the man in black was under heavy fire, albeit that the handguns were less effective at this distance. I saw Pieter running towards the nearest of the Kalashnikovs.

The man in black quickly covered the short distance to his car, firing all the while. Bullets were going everywhere and ricocheting off the car's bodywork. I had him in my sights as he was opening the driver's door. I fired and through the telescopic sight saw him jerk back, hit in the shoulder — damned distance had made all the difference. He was inside his Mercedes before I could fire off a second shot. The car sped forwards, smoke from burning rubber coming in a thick black cloud behind him.

Pieter had the Kalashnikov raised and

aimed at the car. A burst or two would bring the car to a halt and then the man in black was ours for the taking. Pieter pressed the trigger as the rest of us were racing for our assault rifles. I saw him frown and press the trigger again. Nothing happened, The damned Kalashnikov, true to form, had jammed. Pieter threw it to the ground and kicked it away in temper. By the time the rest of us had our rifles the man in black had raced past us and was gone.

I walked to where Jerome and Lucy were lying on the floor. Helped them up. Looked at them both. Lucy seemed like she was in some sort of trance, her eyes staring, no words coming from her mouth. I held her in my arms and hugged her tightly. A thin smile appeared on her lips. She would be all right.

Jerome was shaking. He handed me the gun, holding it by his fingertips as if it was a dead rat he had found. I took it from him and tucked it into my trousers.

'You did well, old man,' I said.

'I couldn't fire the gun, Johnny,' he said. 'It's not in me, in spite of what he'd done. Seems like I have to leave the shooting to men like you.'

'Time for another shot of bourbon,' I said.

He nodded, took out the bottle and took a large gulp. He wiped the top of the bottle with his hand and passed it to me. I raised it in salute to him and took a drink. Maybe time for a celebration later — Lucy was safe and that was the main thing. I'd winged the man in black and maybe that would either put him off for good or take him out of the action for a while.

I led Lucy to the jeep and helped her inside. She wouldn't let go of me. I squashed into the front beside her. Kept her body close to mine. She put her head on my shoulder and I felt her relax.

Everyone else climbed into one or other of our two vehicles and we set off to take Lucy back to the Retreat. Mission accomplished. Well, partly.

* * *

Rafael rushed to meet us, beaming all the while. 'You did it!' he said. 'You did it!'

'We did it,' I corrected. 'Team effort. Jerome deserves the most credit for facing the man in black and then making Lucy safe while the bullets were flying. The only problem is that the man in black got away, although not unscathed. We've put three bullets in him so far and he still keeps getting away. He's a hard man to stop.'

I led Lucy to one of the armchairs and sat

her down. She wouldn't let go of me, so I sat on the arm and held her hand in mine. The others gathered around us and milled about, too high on adrenaline to sit down.

'How are you feeling?' I asked Lucy.

'Sort of spaced out,' she said, slurring her words. 'He made me take pills. Got kinda sleepy afterwards.'

'Did he harm you in any way?' Rafael said.

She shook her head. 'Just kept me doped up. I don't even remember much of what happened. It was the basement of a house somewhere. We drove for about thirty minutes to get there, although he could have been going in circles for all I knew. I think he used chloroform to snatch me. Made me feel sick.' She looked at me with misty eyes. 'I knew you'd come,' she said. 'My knight in shining armour.'

I heard Bull in the background scoffing. 'I hate to spoil the reunion,' he said, 'but at the end of the day the man in black got what he wanted. He got the letters.'

'Not quite,' I said. 'He got *some* letters.'

'Don't see the difference,' Bull said.

'He didn't get the letters he wanted, he got the letters I prepared for him.'

'I'm lost,' Red said. 'I signed the letter and Jerome gave it to him.'

'I signed mine, too,' Rafael said. 'So now

we're committed to selling.'

Time for explanations. Put them out of their misery.

'When I was in town, I got a most helpful girl at the hotel to prepare the letters for me. She photocopied the original letters, but with a blank sheet of paper covering everything but the Crane, Oaks and Crane letterhead. Then she retyped the letters with the subtle addition of the words *do not. I do not agree to sell* etc. Neither of you checked the letters, just scrawled your signatures, and I gambled that all the man in black would do is check that you had both signed. Who's going to read all that legal gobbledygook? Especially when you're facing five guys who are itching to shoot the hell out of you.'

'So we don't have to sell?' Red said.

'Nope. You're not committed to anything. I'd like to see the faces of those who hired the man in black when they realize he's failed against us again. Won't be good for his reputation. Shouldn't wonder if they don't terminate his contract.'

'And send someone else?' Bull asked.

'Maybe.'

'You did it again,' he said. 'Used that maybe word.'

'We need to find out who and why. We're pretty sure the senator is involved, but why?

What's so important that he wants us all out? Is it simply about prejudice? Or is there something else? I feel we're missing something.'

'Silver got played out a century ago,' Jerome said. 'Can't be that. Ain't no oil around here either. And never been a gold rush. My money's on prejudice.'

'And you would know,' Red said. 'Me, too. Plenty of people still don't like a half-breed, even in this day and age. My bet is the senator is one of them.'

'The senator regards us as a bunch of hippies,' Rafael said. 'Lowers the tone of the neighbourhood. Most of which the senator owns.'

'Maybe,' I said.

'Stop doing that,' Bull said. 'And, while we're all here, why didn't you tell us about these fake letters?'

'Because I wanted everything to be realistic. If you had known, you might have reacted differently — like nothing really mattered. It had to seem important, like we were giving up reluctantly, but that we'd still try to get the man in black.'

'If only that Kalashnikov hadn't jammed,' said Pieter. 'He would have been mincemeat.'

'Hate to say I told you so, but I told you so. The Uzi is more reliable — doesn't jam on you at important moments.'

'What do you want?' Pieter said. 'Applause?'

'Would be nice,' I said.

'Let's have a drink to celebrate,' Rafael said. 'You must try our sweetcorn wine. Brew it ourselves from only the finest cobs.'

The prospect didn't thrill me.

'Perhaps later,' Stan said. 'I need to know whether I have to be doing more planning. Is the man in black going to be coming back for me? Play some new trick on us?'

'My guess is that his contract will be rescinded.'

'And that they'll hire someone else?' Red asked.

'And before you answer that question,' Bull said, 'let me advise you not to use the *maybe* word. If I hear it one more time I'm likely to explode.'

'The man in black is finished. Now that Lucy is safe back here we can tell the sheriff what has happened and get the state cops to put out an APB on him. His days are numbered. Kidnapping is a very serious offence. I think he can look forward to a very long spell in prison.'

'In that case,' said Rafael, 'it's sweetcorn wine time.'

I wanted to make a discreet exit, but Lucy still had me in a tight grip. I could see the others frowning and looking at me for guidance. I shrugged my shoulders.

Rafael went into a corner of the room and reappeared with an innocuous-looking bottle of pale yellow liquid. He uncorked it and started to pour into some pottery goblets that were on the table. He passed one to me and I sipped it gingerly. It wasn't as bad as I had feared, which isn't saying much. It was very sweet and had the texture of thick treacle.

'It's good,' I said politely.

'Can I have one?' said Lucy.

'Me, too,' said Cameron.

Rafael looked at Fey, who nodded. 'As it's a special occasion,' she said.

In that case they should have spared the kids. But what the hell, might put them off drinking for good.

Lucy took an experimental sip. Pulled a face. 'Nice,' she said. She squeezed my hand. 'I've been silly, haven't I? Getting all fussed up about you.'

'No need to apologize. I'm flattered.'

'Is she nice, your woman?'

'Very,' I said. 'We're good for each other.'

'She keeps him on the right track,' said Bull. 'Who knows what he'd get up to without her. Doesn't bear thinking about.'

Lucy let go of my hand. 'She's lucky,' she said.

'Some might say that,' Bull said. 'Others . . . '

Lucy giggled.

'Thank you for what you did,' she said. 'I'll try not to get silly again.'

'That's what being young is about,' I said. 'Youth carries with it the licence to be silly. To make mistakes. Plenty of time to be serious when you're grown up. Anyway, I'm flattered.'

'So you should be,' she said.

I downed the wine in one. Fought back a shiver. 'Time we were going,' I said. 'Big day, tomorrow.'

Bull looked at me for clarification.

'Stan, Pieter and I are filling in a pit. Red is taking you to the dentist. I'm fed up with you groaning half the night, and wincing every time you have something hot or cold. You'll get that tooth fixed even if Red has to strap you in the chair and force your mouth open with a crowbar.'

'Be a shame to bother a dentist,' Bull said. 'It might get better on its own.'

'Do you really believe that?'

He considered it. ''Spose not,' he said grudgingly.

'Can you believe it?' I said to Lucy. 'A fully grown man — one who has fought many battles to boot — and he's scared of the dentist.'

'Not scared as such,' he said.

I gave him a withering look.

'Terrified,' he said. 'Bad experience as a kid

— too much sugar cane, too little brushing. Had four teeth taken out in one go. Never fully recovered from it.'

'Do you want a bottle of the sweetcorn wine to take with you?' Rafael asked.

'Too much of a good thing,' I said.

'You'd only be spoiling us,' said Pieter.

'Got to keep a clear head for filling in the pit,' said Stan.

'Got to play bodyguard,' said Red.

'Well, thanks again,' said Rafael. 'For everything. And that goes for all of us.'

'It was nothing,' I said.

'Speak for yourself,' Bull said grumpily.

'You know, I'm really looking forward to tomorrow,' I said. 'Perhaps we should all come and watch. Make an event of it. Film it for posterity.'

'Nothing to fear from the dentist,' Jerome said, 'He's not lost a patient for a year or so now.'

'And I thought us black guys stuck together,' Bull said.

Jerome pointed at me. 'He's been the one who buys me beer and coffees with bourbon in. Sort of divides your loyalties.'

'You're all enjoying this, aren't you,' Bull said to us. 'Just you wait.'

'Enough,' I said, 'or I'll give you an ice cube to suck.'

21

We all enjoyed a late breakfast except for a subdued Bull, who was sharp and irritable when he wasn't being silent. I didn't know which I preferred — both were unnatural for him. He and Red departed for town and the three of us who were left stripped off our shirts and started loading the wheelbarrows with the earth to fill up the pit. It was going to be another hot day, although we'd never had anything else in our time here. We'd be working up a sweat. It would be nice to lose ourselves in some manual labour, not to mention not having to think of the man in black.

It was a slow process. We needed to stop frequently to replace the liquid we were losing. Just as we were starting to make real progress Stan gave a shout. 'Damn!'

'What's the problem?' I asked.

'Ring slipped off my finger. Fell into this damn pit.'

Pieter and I stared into the pit. The words *needle* and *haystack* came to mind.

'Nothing for it but to get in there and dig around,' Pieter said. 'I'd help you, but I have this fear of depths.'

Stan's sense of humour was restricted to jokes about dill pickles, so Pieter's remark went over his head. He jumped down into the pit and started to dig around with his hands like someone who pans for gold does with a sieve, sifting dirt from one part of the pit to the far end, away from where the ring might have landed. Pieter and I stopped and drank some water and peered into the pit for any sign of a sparkle.

After ten minutes Stan gave another shout. 'Got it,' he said triumphantly, holding the ring aloft.

Pieter and I grabbed a hand each and helped Stan climb out of the pit. He polished the ring on a handkerchief and put it in his pocket so as to avoid a repeat of the incident.

'What's that on your hands?' I said. Stan's hands were a dull grey-black with the odd silvery sheen.

'Some sort of stain from digging around in the dirt,' he said. 'It'll wash off.'

'Excitement over,' I said. 'Back to work.'

'I'm starting to envy Bull,' Pieter said, standing up to his full height and rubbing his back. 'Maybe we should take out a patent on a wheelbarrow designed for tall men.'

I tipped another load into the pit and headed back to the piles of earth near the ranch house. I made a mental note to call Pa Blenkenstein and get him to come over and collect the digger.

We stopped for coffee and to fill up our water bottles. Stan washed his hands, but the stain stubbornly refused to go. He shrugged and drank his coffee greedily, taking large gulps and sighing with satisfaction. It was good coffee, Jamaican Blue Mountain like we had on St Jude, too good not to savour.

Stan looked at us. 'Well,' he said. 'When are we getting back to work? Can't be seen here sitting down and sipping coffee when Red and Bull get back, They'll think we've been taking it easy all morning.'

'OK.' I sighed. 'Coffee break over.'

We got up and wheeled our barrows to the diminishing pile of earth. Another few hours and we should have it done, especially if Red and Bull helped as well. We lifted our spades and got back into sweat mode.

It was another hour before Red and Bull got back. Bull was all smiles.

'Didn't have to take it out,' he said. 'Just drilled and filled.'

'What did you say?' I asked.

'Drilled and filled. Why?'

A cold shiver ran down my spine. Hell. 'We have been such fools,' I said.

'Speak for yourself,' Bull said.

I turned to Red. 'Have you got a university near here?'

He shook his head. 'Got a college halfway to Fort Stockton. Best I can do.'

'Excuse me then, guys, but I'll have to leave you to fill in the pit. Things to do, places to go, people to see.'

They looked at me as if I was mad. If my theory was right, they'd see me in a better light soon. I showered quickly, washed off the sweat and earth, then dressed in clean clothes. I went to the kitchen and fetched a brown-paper bag. Red threw the keys to the jeep to me and I was off, adrenaline pumping.

* * *

The drive took about thirty minutes. The college was a modern brick-and-glass building, two storeys high. The building was surrounded by grassy lawns with students lying back, catching a few rays and trying to look like they were thinking deep thoughts. Mostly they were smoking and talking — nothing much changes. There was a spare space in the car park marked 'Principal' and I slotted the jeep in there. I walked up the steps and entered an air-conditioned atrium filled with large pots of tropical plants in some hydroponic material. The whole area was green, light and airy, a far cry from my days at school. There was a receptionist's desk facing the entrance, behind which sat a woman with red hair, too much make-up and a bosom that looked like it would make it difficult for her to stand up straight without falling forwards; I started to wonder whether it was a requirement of a receptionist's job. Maybe I'd just been unlucky with my random sample of two — or maybe lucky, I suppose. I approached her, trying to look her in the eyes and appear confident at the same time. She gave me a manufactured smile.

'I'm looking for a geologist,' I said.

'What's that?' she said.

'You know, rocks and stuff.'

'Mr Meacham teaches geography. Will that do?'

Geology, geography, what's the difference, she seemed to be saying. Maybe she was right.

'OK. I'd like to talk with Mr Meacham.'

She looked at her computer screen and frowned. 'He's teaching class until three,' she said.

'I'll wait.'

'Do you have an appointment?'

'Just ring him and tell him I'd like to contribute to his next field trip.'

'We don't do field trips. Can't afford it.'

'Well, you can now.'

'Take a seat,' she said. 'I'll text him.'

I sat down in a faux-leather chair and looked at the pile of magazines on the black coffee table. There were a few copies of a prospectus for the college and a small collection of learned journals, presumably featuring articles by the staff — didn't seem much point in them otherwise. I went for the prospectus and soon learnt more than I ever wanted to know about the college. At a little past three a tall man in his late thirties with long unkempt hair, jeans and a check jacket with elbow patches walked over to me.

'You wanted to see me?'

'Johnny Silver,' I said. 'I need to talk geology. Can you handle that?'

He nodded.

'After we've talked I'd like to make a donation for your next field trip, or books if you prefer. Whatever you want.'

He nodded again, more thoughtfully this time.

'Follow me, Mr Silver.'

He led me up a flight of stairs and along a long narrow corridor with an insipid green carpet on the floor until we reached a room with his name on a plaque on the door. He opened the door and ushered me inside.

My confidence grew. I'd found the right man. The office was a mess of paper strewn over every surface — desk, side table, chairs, window ledge, piled on the floor. This was a room of a guy who pretty much knew everything, certainly seemed to read everything.

'What do you know about the geology of the Pecos?' I asked.

'Nothing that's interesting. Was some silver there a while back, but that was soon played out — not high enough a content to make it worth mining. Why?'

I picked up the brown-paper bag and handed it to him. 'I'd like to know what this is,' I said.

'Came from the Pecos?'

I nodded.

He peered into the bag, dipped his hand in and drew out some of the earth. Rubbed it between his fingers. Looked at the stain that formed.

'I'll need to run some tests,' he said.

'I can wait,' I said.

'Make yourself comfortable. Can I get you some coffee?'

'That would be good.'

He left the room with the bag in his right hand. Five minutes later a young girl brought me some coffee on a tray with cream and sugar and a bone china cup and saucer. They were pushing the boat out. I could get used to this, but I'd lose credibility points with the others.

He came back an hour later, smiling. Good sign. He sat himself down in the chair, leaned back and looked across at me.

'You heard of rhodium?' he asked.

I shook my head.

'Well, that's what you got.'

It sounded like a disease. 'Is that good or bad?' I said.

'Very good,' he said. 'Let me tell you about rhodium.'

Lecture time. I was all ears. 'You might want to dumb it down a bit,' I said.

'I'm a college lecturer. What do you think I do all day?'

'Silly of me,' I said.

'Rhodium,' he said. 'Knew that was what was in the bag before I even did the tests — stains.' He showed me his fingers, stained like Stan's. 'Atomic number 45, one of the noble metals — inert, won't corrode or react with anything. Usually found in small quantities along with other metals — silver mainly. Worldwide output only 25 tonnes a year.'

'Wow. So it's valuable?'

'In 2007 it was worth eight times as much as gold, 450 times as much as silver and 27,250 times copper. Prices have dropped back a bit, but it's still worth around 2,750 dollars an ounce.'

'Wow, again,' I said, exhaling. 'What's it used for?'

'Mostly for catalytic converters. Small amounts for jewellery, too. Plate over white gold to enhance its appearance — the shine — and on silver to prevent it tarnishing. The world can't get enough of the stuff.'

It all made sense now. The final pieces of the puzzle were fitting together.

'About this field trip?' he said. 'I was thinking of taking the geography students to Iceland, study the volcanoes and the places where the two tectonic plates meet. Would be good for them.'

'Go the long way round the world, if you like. I — or more precisely, my soon-to-be rich friend — will foot the bill. I'll get him to send a cheque in the next couple of weeks.'

'Very generous,' he said, 'How much of this rhodium does your friend have?'

'Wealth beyond the dreams of avarice,' I said. 'I would guess there's a major seam of rhodium running through his ranch.'

'Hallelujah,' he said.

'Hallelujah indeed.' I stretched out my hand and we shook. 'Many thanks, Mr Meacham. You don't know how grateful I am.'

'I think I can guess,' he said, smiling.

22

I called Pa Blenkenstein first thing the next morning and arranged for him to come round and pick up his digger at ten o'clock. I made all the necessary arrangements and brewed some coffee. I carried the pot through to the dining table, leaving the kitchen door slightly open. I poured some coffee into mugs, passed them around to everybody and sat to wait for his arrival. I was looking forward to this. It's not often you can show off your deductive capabilities. For effect, I wore the Browning conspicuously in the shoulder holster over a T-shirt, no jacket.

I heard a vehicle outside and went to the window; Ma Blenkenstein was dropping her husband off. He went across to the digger, climbed on board and paused. I had the keys.

I walked to the door and opened it, cried out a welcome. Pa approached me.

'You'll have some coffee,' I said.

'I better be getting back.'

'You'll have some coffee,' I said firmly.

He looked at me uncertainly. 'OK,' he said.

I ushered him through the door and gestured at a chair at the table. There were nods from around the table. Bull stood up and went to the door, leaned against it — no escape. I poured Pa a coffee and placed it in front of him along with the sugar bowl and a small jug of cream. I took a chair opposite him.

'I want to posit a theory,' I said.

In the background I could see Bull mouth *posit*, smile and shake his head.

'I want to tell you a story,' I said. 'It's a story of a couple of old folks. Farmers who scratch a living from their spread. It's a hard life, but they have known no other and have no hope of a different future.'

'What's this about?' he said. 'I ain't got time to listen to fairy stories.'

'Bear with me,' I said. 'This is no fairy story.' I took a sip of coffee to increase the tension. I saw beads of sweat forming on Pa's forehead. 'Then one day everything changes. Their one and only son dies. They're grief-stricken and wonder how life will be without him. Sound familiar?'

He gave a grunt, which I took to be a grudging answer in the affirmative.

'This old couple,' I continued, 'decide to bury their son on their land rather than in a graveyard in a church of a different faith. They start to dig. How am I doing so far?'

He made a move to get up. Red stretched

across an arm and pushed him back in the chair. 'Be rude to leave before Johnny's finished his story. You ain't going nowhere.'

'So they dig,' I repeated so as not to lose the flow. 'And they notice something funny about the soil — it glitters in places. They think they've struck silver like in the old days. Their eyes begin to light up. This could be the answer to all their prayers.'

I took another sip of coffee and scanned his face. There was fear there now. The sweat was beginning to run faster, too.

'So one of them, let's say it's Pa, says we need to get this checked out. They prepare a sample and take it to an assay office somewhere, Dallas maybe; I'm guessing, but some place big where the guys know their stuff. Bingo! Hallelujah! It's not silver, it's rhodium. They haven't ever heard of that, but the assayer tells them it's one of the rarest metals and the price is sky high. They extend their mortgage at the bank, buy a digger and see that there's a big seam of it running diagonally through their spread. They've made it. A fortune just sitting in their own land, waiting to be dug up and cashed. But this is where they make their first mistake — they get greedy. Whose idea was it, Pa — you or Ma?'

'I don't know what you're talking about.

Rhodium — what the hell is that?'

'Oh, well. Let's say it's your idea. You start to think: 'Wait a minute. This band of rhodium seems like it goes through Red's land and the Retreat, too. There's more money to be made here. Buy up their land and their fortune grows three-fold. But they hit a snag. They don't have the money. The bank won't lend them any more — they won't be able to keep up with the higher mortgage payments. What are they going to do? Can't let that potential huge sum slip through their fingers. So they have their second idea. Involve someone who does have the money and split the profit — half's better than none.' I turned my attention towards Red and the other guys. 'Help me out here, boys. Who do we know who's got plenty of money and no conscience? Someone who wouldn't consider Red and the people from the Retreat as being 'proper' citizens worthy of respect and who deserve to be cheated out of what is rightfully theirs? Who do we know who fits the bill?'

'Senator O'Hara,' they chorused.

I nodded my head. 'Good old fine upstanding Senator O'Hara. One who likes to live dangerously — calls Bull 'boy'. He's got big ambitions. The White House beckons. The money from the rhodium will kick start his campaign fund. Manna from heaven. So they start to make approaches to Red and Rafael. No dice. Rafael and his people like living there, got no reason to move. And as for Red, it's the first real home he's ever had. Why should he move on?'

Pa shuffled in the chair, started clenching his hands tightly, the sweat running off him like a mountain stream. He was beginning to crack. Any minute now it would all spill out and there would be no holding back the dam.

'The senator knows people — that's part of the benefit of being a senator: you come across lots of people, good and bad. He knows the man in black, or he's heard of him from a friend or a friend of a friend. Whatever. The man in black can solve all their problems. No one can get the best of the man in black. Red and Rafael were as good as out the door.' I picked up the coffee pot and poured myself some more. 'And then we show up. Best laid plans and all that. They hadn't bargained for any resistance. The man in black starts off low by poisoning the water, frightening the ranch hands, even shooting a bullet at me to try to warn us off. But Red's stubborn, and his friends even more so — try moving Bull when his mind's made up.'

'You got that right,' Bull said.

'So the man in black starts to escalate

matters. Hires a bunch of bikers to beat the stubbornness out of us. We beat them instead. So it's more bikers and we beat them, too. And then he sinks really low — kidnaps Lucy.'

'And we fool him with some phoney letters,' Red said. 'And nearly kill him. Send him off with his tail between his legs and a bullet in his shoulder.'

'How have I done, Pa? Anything I missed out?'

'They didn't deserve it,' Pa said. 'Red won the ranch in a poker game. Didn't have to work hard for it like the rest of us. It wasn't fair. And as for the hippies, they don't need it. Bunch of good-for-nothings. Probably spend it all on drugs.' He looked me in the eye. 'We slaved all those years. We deserved it.'

'And you were willing to go along with the senator's plans. Beat up people, kidnap a young girl, kill a few of us while you're about it?'

He shrugged.

'Don't you shrug at me,' I said angrily. 'You knew exactly what you were doing. You deserve everything that you get. I only wish that you were younger so that you could spend more of your life in jail.'

'How did you put it together?' he asked. 'Where did we slip up?'

'That's where Bull comes into the picture.'

'Proud to be of service,' he said.

'Bull and his rotten tooth. The dentist didn't have to take it out. He just drilled it. It struck me that, in these modern times, you don't dig for a well, you drill it. So what were you doing with that digger? Checking out where the seam of rhodium ran, that's what. What beats me is why you lent us the digger in the first place. Big risk we might come to the right conclusion.'

'Thought it might look odd if I refused you. And, let's face it, Red is an Injun.' I could sense another hole being dug here. 'They don't have the brains to work anything out. And as for you, well, I never put you down as being smart.'

I think I would have preferred to be called an Injun.

'Damn digger,' he said. Then he became pensive. He leaned back in the chair. Looked me in the eye. 'Seems like you've got nothing to go on but guesses. No hard evidence. It'll be your word against mine. And who are they going to believe? An honest God-fearing man like me, or a bunch of mercenaries?'

I got up from the table, walked across to the kitchen door. Opened it wide.

'You can come out now, Sheriff,' I said.

'Thank you, boys. Getting a bit claustrophobic in there.' He smiled at Pa Blenkenstein.

Not a nice smile. His eyes looked like those of a cobra before it rears up and bites you. 'Well, Pa. I've always wanted to say this. Ah ha, the game is up.'

'In England nowadays we say 'You're nicked.'

'I stand corrected. You're nicked. Why don't we take a ride to town and you give me a statement. Then I might persuade the judge to go easy on you. And your wife, too. Shame for her to finish up in prison. You might not ever see each other again.'

The sheriff was smarter than he looked. Knew where to hit the hardest. He took Pa by the arm and led him to the door. Just before they went out he turned around and said to us, 'Give me a couple of hours and then join me at my office. I think we've got another call to make.'

23

We stood in a line facing the sheriff in his office. We were wearing our shoulder holsters under lightweight jackets and stood as much to attention as such a disparate group could manage. Tucker held a Bible in his hand, although we were not quite sure why. I suspected he didn't know either.

'Repeat after me,' he said. 'I do solemnly swear . . . '

'I do solemnly swear . . . ' we chorused.

'That I will do my duty . . . '

'That I will do my duty . . . '

He looked up at us helplessly. 'Hell, I've never done this before.'

'Hell, I've never done this before.'

'Don't do that.'

'Don't do that.'

By this time we were doubled up with laughter.

'If you don't stop that, I'll put you in the cell with Pa Blenkenstein.'

'If you . . . '

We looked at each other. Time to stop teasing him. After all, he was helping us. He was making us all special deputies so that

O'Hara couldn't refuse to let us into his house. Not one of us wanted to miss the climax of all our efforts, the denouement of our stay in Texas.

'Don't I get a badge or something?' Red asked.

The sheriff looked around, saw some yellow Post-it notes on his desk. Peeled off one, wrote 'Deputy' on it and stuck it to Red's jacket. 'Happy now?' he said.

'Just what I always wanted,' Red said. 'Let's go.'

We followed the sheriff's car out to the senator's ranch. Stood in a group at the front door while waiting for Jackson to answer it. When he did, he stared at me. I got the impression he knew what was coming. Maybe not any details, but that he would be looking for a new job by the end of the day. I felt sorry for him. Hoped he'd find somewhere else with someone who would treat him with respect.

'We'll come straight in,' the sheriff said. 'No need to tell the senator that we're here.'

'Yes, sir,' said Jackson. 'Follow me, sir. This way, sir.'

He led us through to the garden. O'Hara and Slim were sitting at the table under the shade of a white-fringed umbrella. There was a jug of something cool between them, a bucket of ice and two highball glasses half-full, or half-empty, depending on your point of view. The senator looked at us as a group, focused on Bull and Red and jumped to his feet, his face red with anger.

'What the hell are you doing here?' he shouted. 'Jackson, show these men out.'

''Fraid not,' said the sheriff. 'This is official.' He waved his hand in our direction. 'These are my five special deputies.'

'Who'd love nothing more than to find you resisting arrest.' I opened my jacket to reveal the shoulder holster. 'We're packing,' I said, 'You behave yourself, Senator.'

Jackson turned round and started to walk back inside the house.

'You should stay, Jackson,' I said. 'Might learn something about human nature.'

'I'm well versed in that already, sir.'

'How about greed?'

''Specially that, sir. But I will stay.'

'I call the shots around here, Jackson. Leave us.'

'I think I'll stay, sir.'

He didn't say 'if you don't mind', simply moved to the side so that he could see both O'Hara and us in his field of vision. He removed his white gloves and put them in his pocket. The spell — the thrall — he'd been under here had just broken. It was probably the first time that Jackson had said anything for himself, rather than maintaining silence, acquiescing to O'Hara's whims and bowing and licking.

'What's the meaning of this?' O'Hara said, sitting back down. 'You'll pay for this, Tucker. Don't you forget that I'm also the mayor of this town and *I* appoint the sheriff.'

'At the moment,' Tucker said. 'There are some big changes coming.'

I picked up a spare chair, turned it round and sat with my legs straddling the seat so that I was facing O'Hara, and looked pretty cool in the process. I knew Bull would make me pay for it later, but it was worth it to see the senator's face — if the veins bulging got any worse, then O'Hara would have a heart attack.

'Get rid of this bunch of thugs, Sheriff.'

'You've got a big mouth, Senator,' said Bull. 'Goes with the territory, I suppose.'

'What do you want?' he said.

'I want to see you squirm, Senator,' I said.

'That goes for me, too,' said Bull.

'And the rest of us,' said Red.'

'Always been partial to a bit of squirming,' said Pieter.

'When you can't eat another dill pickle, then it's time to give in,' said Stan enigmatically.

'My lawyers — '

'I know. Crane, Oaks and Crane. And they're going to sue the arses off us.'

'Asses,' Tucker corrected. 'I have a sworn statement, Senator, from Pa Blenkenstein implicating you in a series of crimes. I'll settle for conspiracy to kidnap a minor while we piece together everything else.'

'I'll take my leave, Sheriff,' said Slim.

'You stay right where you are,' said Tucker. 'We haven't figured out your part in all this yet.'

'I only acted as a go-between,' Slim said. 'Between the senator and the man in black.'

'Hold your tongue, Slim,' said O'Hara. 'If we say nothing, then they can't make anything stick.'

'It's too late for that, Senator,' I said. 'You're finished.'

'I'll testify,' Slim said. 'I was just obeying orders. I didn't know what the man in black would do.'

'Ah, the man in black,' I said. 'How much did he cost you, Senator? Because you didn't get your money's worth.'

'I refuse to answer any of your questions. I plead the fifth amendment.'

'We could rough him up a bit,' said Bull.

'You lay a finger on me and I'll . . . '

'You'll do what?' said Bull. 'Retch? Because

being a bigot's going to get you into even more trouble.'

I turned to Slim. 'Help us catch the man in black and the sheriff will do whatever he can for you.'

Slim looked at the sheriff. Tucker nodded.

'I'll help where I can,' Slim said. 'But it's not much. I don't even know his name.'

'How do you get in touch with him?' I asked.

'Ring a cellphone. It's his answering service. He then gets back to you.'

'How many times have you met him?' Tucker said.

'Just the once at the very beginning of the contract. Met him in a park at Fort Stockton. Stood on a bridge over the water feeding the ducks, like in the spy movies. Explained exactly what we — I mean the senator — wanted. Handed over half the fee in cash. Brown-paper bag. You know how it works?'

'I can guess,' Tucker said.

'Do you still owe him the other half of the money?' I said.

'Not due until we had the land.'

'Better hope that the man in black sees it that way, too,' I said. 'Otherwise prison won't be the worst that happens to you.'

'I told you, I was just the go-between.'

I turned my attention to the senator. He

was looking calmer, like he was planning something that would get him out of trouble.

'So we got Pa's statement and Slim's testimony. Why not confess, Senator?' I said. 'You might need protection. The man in black may feel he wasn't fully briefed, that the contract was a lot trickier than you said. He may feel he's due the rest of the money. I wouldn't like to be in your shoes.'

'If you were in my shoes I'd burn them.'

Boy, did he know how to make matters worse!

'Not going to look good for a prospective presidential candidate,' I said. 'Mind you, you'll get a mugshot for free; use it on your campaign posters.'

'It needn't come to that,' he said. He turned to Tucker. 'I'm sure we can reach an arrangement, Sheriff,' he said. 'I'm a wealthy man. Name your price to get rid of these good for nothings and to drop the charges against me.'

'I have six witnesses' — he looked at Slim who nodded — 'make that seven witnesses that you just tried to bribe a police officer. You're in a hole, Senator. Stop digging.'

'Think about it, Sheriff. You could retire, live the life of luxury.'

'Enough,' Tucker said. 'I'm arresting you on a charge of conspiracy to kidnap a minor and accessory to the act.'

Tucker went through the formal caution and then went over to O'Hara. He took out a pair of handcuffs and clipped one half around the senator's right wrist.

'Is this really necessary?' O'Hara asked. 'I'm no danger to you. On the contrary, I could make life sweet for you.'

'I said stop digging, Senator. Now give me your other wrist.'

O'Hara looked like a child who had lost his favourite toy. It was beginning to sink in. There was no way out. All his plans had turned to dust. His shot at the presidency was over. Even if his lawyers managed to get him off a conspiracy charge by some legal trickery, he wouldn't get the nomination, let alone a single vote. His fine career path was now a dream — make that a nightmare. And the best part of it was that he deserved it. A lot of people would be happy to see him fall.

Tucker placed the handcuff around the senator's left wrist and led him through the house towards his car.

'Sorry, Jackson,' I said. 'We didn't mean you to suffer.'

'I think it's time to retire,' he said. 'I can keep Jerome company on that porch. Drink a little beer and talk about old times.' He looked at me and nodded. 'You did the right thing,' he said. 'No one's been prepared to stand up to the senator. He needed to be taken down a peg or three. Boy, is this gonna cause a stink.' He smiled. 'Can't wait. I'm gonna enjoy every minute of this.'

I shook his hand. Said, 'Look after yourself,' and walked to the sheriff's car. I'd travel back to town with him. I had other things to do.

24

It was time to start saying goodbyes. Our work was over and soon we would all be going back to our own lives, the fellowship broken for a while. We'd all be back together, I hoped, for my wedding to Anna. A quieter gathering then, no one opposing us, no wrongs to right. Simply enjoy the moment.

I walked along the main street back from the sheriff's office. He'd been helpful again. Oh, how I had misjudged him when we first met. Maybe I hadn't been all wrong; maybe he'd changed. Realized that the law had to be without fear or favour. That no man, however powerful, was outside the law.

Jerome was sitting in the rocking-chair, looking melancholy.

'You're packing heavy today,' he said, gesturing at my bulging jacket. 'I hear you got the senator.'

'News travels fast here.'

'Especially when it's good news.'

'What else do you hear?'

'How Jackson's gonna take a well-deserved retirement. How he's free now. Don't have to take any crap any more — pardon my

French. Can stand tall. Be proud of what he is rather than being reminded all the time of what he isn't.'

'What else do you hear?'

'How the town's gonna be rich again, now we got this rhodium stuff. It's the big time from now on — hotel's gonna be too small. Maybe there won't be room for an old man.'

'There will always be room for you.'

'That's what the boss said. Local colour, he called it.'

'And they said Americans didn't do irony.'

'So you'll be riding off now,' he said. 'Gonna miss you.'

'One last beer?'

He nodded. 'Be good,' he said.

I went inside and got two cold beers and a dish of peanuts. Took them out to the porch. Handed one to Jerome.

'Don't need the peanuts any more,' he said.

'Never too early to start training,' I said.

I unzipped my jacket and took hold of the sleepy bundle. Held it aloft for Jerome to see. 'Cute or what?' I said, passing the puppy to him.

A tear came to his eye.

'He's never going to be 'dog',' I said, 'but he needs some love. Feels like you're the guy to give him that.'

'Reckon so,' he said, taking the puppy from

me and stroking it gently. 'Good to have company on the porch again. He's a fine dog. And you're a fine man. Will I see you again?'

'Reckon so,' I said. 'I'm not just going to ride off into the sunset. Red will need keeping on the straight and narrow while he builds his fortune. And I'm kind of going to miss this place. There's good folks here. Be proud to call them my friends.'

'Be proud to be your friend,' he said, holding back a tear. 'Gonna call the dog Silver, like you. He's gonna be precious to me. Come back and see him when he's fully grown.'

'And when he can catch peanuts,' I said. 'Goodbye, old man.'

I turned and walked away. I hoped he would still be here on my next visit. The town would be less rich without him. And the dog. Always got to be a dog there. They'd make a fine pair.

* * *

I walked back to the ranch. It took an hour, but that gave me plenty of time for thinking. When I arrived back I saddled up Shadow and rode off to take the cross-country route we'd created to the Retreat. I was going to miss this horse. No riding to be done on St

Jude and there certainly wasn't a horse to match Shadow. I gave him his head and, after a brief canter to get his muscles working, we galloped the rest of the way. We both felt free.

Rafael and Fey welcomed me and offered me a glass of home-made lemonade. It was good, just the right level of sweetness. There might be something to their way of life after all. It certainly beat the sweetcorn brew, but then that would not be difficult.

We sat in three of the battered armchairs. Fey was wearing a simple shift dress in iridescent blue that matched her eyes. Rafael had on a white long-sleeved shirt and white drawstring trousers. He refilled my glass and nodded his head at me.

'You've given us a pretty pickle of a problem.' He sounded like Stan, but with a lighter tone to his voice. 'What are we going to do with all the money from the rhodium?'

'Nice problem to have,' I said.

'It might change our way of life,' he said. 'Will we be able to coexist with the mining that will be going on? Should we sell the land for a big fat profit and move on to somewhere that will be quieter?'

'Maybe you can have the mining done in stages so that you can rotate your fields and minimize the disruption. With the money you will make, you could expand the Retreat.

Cater for more lost souls.'

'That would be good,' said Fey. 'There's so much good work to be done in this country of ours.'

'I must say I'm disappointed with the Blenkensteins,' said Rafael. 'I thought they were good Christians. That they wouldn't have the sins of envy and greed. The rhodium would have transformed their lives, but they weren't satisfied with that. Now look what has happened to them.'

'Maybe the judge will be lenient and take their age into consideration. After all, it was O'Hara who hired the man in black and was prepared to do anything to get his hands on more land with rhodium.'

'Perhaps we could speak up for them,' said Fey. 'Show there's no hard feelings.'

'That would be a kind thing to do,' I said. 'There really should be more people like you around. I know Red would be sorry if you decide to leave — he's very fond of Cameron, you know. She would benefit from having a mentor. Someone who had the same background as her and the experience of making mistakes and learning from them.'

'Perhaps we should stick around,' Fey said. 'See how it pans out before making any life-changing decisions.'

'As Johnny says,' said Rafael, 'it's a nice

problem to have. I don't know how to thank you.'

'Just carry on doing what you're doing,' I said. 'And more of it. The world needs more people like you — gentle, kind, considerate for others. You're a good example for the rest of us.'

'And you, too,' he said. 'When I heard you were a bunch of mercenaries I was expecting the worst. You don't fit the stereotype.'

'Whatever you do in life,' I said, 'you should do for a reason. Money's not a good enough reason. It's people that count — but you know that. Justice is important, too. Defend the little guy in his battle with guys like the senator. It too often seems that if we don't fight on their side, then nobody will.' I stood up. 'That's too much philosophizing for one day.'

Rafael shook me by my hand. Fey gave me a big hug. 'You come back soon,' she said. 'Especially if you feel the need to get away from the harsh realities of the world for a while.' There was a tear in her eye. 'We're going to miss you.'

'And me you. Is Lucy around?'

'She's in the stables,' Fey said.

'I'll stop off there on my way back. Look after yourselves.'

'And the same to you,' Rafael said.

Lucy was grooming her horse, long strokes brushing its hair so its coat shone. She looked up as I entered and gave me a big smile.

'Have you got time for one last ride?' I said.

She nodded and swallowed as if holding back an emotion. Maybe this wasn't a good idea. She fixed reins on her horse and led it out into the sunshine.

I climbed on to Shadow and we headed north towards the mountains. We rode side by side and then she stopped. I turned Shadow around and waited for her to say what was bothering her.

'Do you really have to go?' she said.

'It's time to return to our own lives. Our work here is done.'

'Not all of it,' she said. 'What about me?'

'What if I say you can come and visit with Anna and me?'

'Will I like her?'

'Yes. You can't help but like her.'

'I suppose so,' she said. 'You seem to have good judgement.'

'Maybe a lot is down to luck.'

She shook her head. 'No. You don't give yourself credit for the things you do and your reasons for doing them.'

'Is this a fourteen-year-old talking?'

She laughed. It sounded hollow. 'I've grown up a lot in these past few weeks. The things that have happened will live with me for the rest of my life. I hope I'll always have someone like you looking out for me. My knight in shining armour.'

I shook my head. 'That's something I can't live up to. I've done some bad things, killed a lot of people.'

'Did they deserve to die?'

I thought about it for a moment or two. 'Yes. They were bad people.'

'Then it's good things that you've done. Lancelot killed bad people, too.'

'And he stole Arthur's wife.'

'Galahad then. You can be my Galahad. Pure in heart. The best of the knights.'

'I'm flattered, but that description doesn't fit either. I've a lot of faults, some I'm ashamed to admit to. I hope you find your Galahad some time in the future. But don't be too hard on those who will love you. Galahad is a hard act to follow.'

'As are you, Johnny Silver. I'll never forget you.'

'Never's a long time. The memory will fade, to be replaced by others. Sometimes in life it's better not to look back.'

'Not with these memories. I'll always treasure them.'

'I think you're right. You have grown up a lot in the last few weeks. I wish you a good life, Lucy. You deserve it.'

She turned her horse round and started to ride back. 'Goodbye, Johnny,' she shouted as she began to fade into the distance. It was a good way to part.

* * *

Red and I went to the hospital. Jesse was sitting up in bed, his arm in plaster, his ribs strapped. The bruises had receded a little and he looked far better than I expected. His teeth had a gap where two had been knocked out, but I presumed that that could be fixed.

We updated him on everything that had happened in his absence and he gave us a thoughtful look.

'So the man in black got away,' he said. 'Not good news.'

'He won't trouble us again. Got nothing to gain by it — his paymaster is in jail and would hardly be in the mood to settle what he doesn't owe for a contract that was never fulfilled. Would have been nice to catch him, but he'll make a slip sooner or later.'

Jesse considered this and his expression changed to a smile.

'They're letting me out tomorrow,' he said. 'Nothing else they can do for me. Would it be OK if I came back to work? Be a bit restricted with what I can do, but I'd get bored on my own.'

'Got a new job for you,' Red said. 'Foreman. Broken arm won't affect what you can do as that. A reward for your loyalty and compensation for what you've been through.'

'Thanks, Red,' he said. 'I won't let you down.'

'There'll be plenty to do,' I said. 'Mixing cattle-ranching and rhodium-mining is not going to be easy. Don't want one to spoil the other.'

'Your first job is to recruit some more hands,' Red said. 'Bring us back up in numbers.'

He gave a rueful smile and shook his head. 'I can dine out on this story for years. If anyone believes me, that is.'

'Too fine a story not to be told,' I said. 'We're leaving tomorrow. It's been good knowing you.'

'And you. Maybe you'll come back some day?'

'Who knows?' I said.

25

We had a visit from the sheriff early the next morning. We made a fresh pot of coffee and sat around the table, thinking of our imminent departure. We didn't need to leave until early afternoon, but I guessed that time would drag. Sometimes it's best not to have to say goodbye. I didn't need anyone getting sentimental — I couldn't trust my own reaction.

'We found his Mercedes,' Tucker said between sips of coffee. 'He'd abandoned it about twenty miles away. Made out something was wrong — put the hood up and stood there looking down. Some poor guy stopped to help. He's now in hospital. The man in black took his car. That was found abandoned, too. Looks like he took a train. Where to, we don't know.' He turned to me. 'That's not the worst of it. Mercedes is registered to a Marty Hamilton at an address in Denver. The address doesn't exist. Neither does Marty Hamilton. No record of that name exists that comes close to his age.'

'Only to be expected,' I said. 'He's a professional. Hardly likely to use his real name.'

'Vanished into the wide blue yonder,' said Bull. 'Not good.'

'He's unlikely to show up anywhere near us,' said Red. 'No one paying his fee any more.'

'Would have been a better ending if he'd been caught,' said Pieter.

'I don't like unfinished business,' said Stan, our man who loved the neat and tidy.

'Not much of a description to go on,' Tucker said. 'All he's got to do is change the colour of his suit and take off his mirrored sunglasses and we've got nothing to go on.'

'He'll show up somewhere,' I said. 'He's got to eat. Got to work to eat. He'll be looking for another contract.'

'Guess you're right,' Tucker said. 'And this time there won't be you guys to thwart him.'

Thwart? Maybe there were still deeper roots to his personality.

'Gonna be kinda quiet without you guys around,' he said.

'Not for long,' I said. 'Pretty soon you'll have all the workers mining for the rhodium. Construction workers, too — men to build places to stay and the infrastructure to deal with the rhodium after it comes out of the ground. Town's going to be buzzing again. Do you think you can handle it?'

'If I can't, I'll give you a call.'

'You know you can always rely on Red, if you need him. Town's going to need a new mayor — you could do worse.'

'Hang on,' said Red. 'Do you mind not planning out my life for me? I might not want the responsibility.'

'Be good for everyone — especially Cameron — to see a half-breed running the show.'

'Now you're playing on my heartstrings.'

'Hit a man where it hurts,' Bull said. 'You should be used to him by now.'

'Don't give away all my secrets,' I said.

'Time for me to be going,' Tucker said. 'Got a town to police.'

He pulled out a small package from his jacket pocket. Something wrapped in brown paper. 'I owe you these,' he said. He unwrapped the paper and handed out something shiny to each of us. It was a badge that said 'Deputy' on it. 'Had someone pick them up from a toy shop. Still, it's the thought that counts.'

I pinned the badge to my T-shirt; the others followed suit.

He turned to me. 'You know, you're not a bad man when you stop acting the wise guy.'

'I'll take that as a compliment,' I said.

'The last thing he needs,' said Bull, 'is someone paying him compliments. Head won't get through the door.'

''Bye, guys,' Tucker said. 'Watch your backs.'

* * *

We sat one last time on the porch, sipping cold beers in a manner that could only be called subdued.

'We'll meet again for my wedding,' I said. 'Better fix it soon before the baby arrives. Good to have everything legitimate.'

'Can't wait,' said Red. 'Seems like every time I meet you I turn out richer.'

'In that case you better come to me next,' said Stan. 'Give my hotel and restaurant a kick start.' He paused. 'Forgot to tell you, Red, but I'm taking your cook. When you've found a replacement she's going to join me.'

'As a cook?' Pieter said. 'Beautiful girl like that deserves more.'

Stan blushed. 'Let's see what the future brings. Don't want to rush things.'

'Don't want to delay either,' I said. 'In this life we've proved that you have to take your opportunities when they present themselves.'

'Not content with planning Red's life, you have to move on to mine,' Stan said.

'How about you, Pieter?' I said. 'What will you be doing?'

'Back to the personalized high-end safari business. It's the kind of life I like — freedom, the thrill of the wild — what you'll see that day, how they'll react. Clients are mostly good people, treat me with respect. Mind you,' he said, 'I'll have to watch my weight from now on. I don't want another punishing fitness regime from Bull when we next meet up.'

I looked at the remains of the apple tree. 'We were lucky with that tree,' I said. 'I doubt whether we could pull that off a second time.'

'Didn't put him off, though, did it?' said Bull. 'Thought all he needed to do was overwhelm us with numbers.'

'We're an easy bunch to underestimate,' said Pieter. 'Old-fashioned values, old-fashioned skills. We'd have fitted in well in the old Wild West.'

'Is that what we are,' I said. 'An anachronism?' Bull looked at me and shook his head — *showing off* is probably what he was thinking. 'Something living outside its time? Are we the new dinosaurs? Will guys like us cease to exist in the future? Be replaced by people who don't care or don't have the skills to do something about things? To make a difference?'

'Too heavy for me, man,' said Bull. 'All I want to do is get back to St Jude and be with my family. And have another beer in the meantime.' He stood up. Went inside. Came back with five more beers. Handed them around. 'Let's toast a successful mission,' he said, 'rather than getting melancholy.'

'I'll drink to that,' said Red.

'You'll drink to anything,' I said. 'But it's a good idea. Cheers.' I looked out over his land towards the mountains. There wasn't a cloud in the sky. The fields were a rich green, shining in the rays of he sun. 'Hope your luck holds. This really is God's land. Are you going to settle down here for good?'

He nodded. 'Like to find a good woman to join me, though. It can be lonely out here, even with the ranch hands being around most of the time. Yeah,' he said. 'Time to settle down.'

'There's always Fey,' I said. 'She'd make a good wife. Pretty, too.'

'Will you stop trying to plan out my life. Anyway,' he said, 'I don't think I could cope with the diet, or the sweetcorn wine.' He shuddered, involuntarily emphasizing the point.

I looked at my watch. Nearly time to go. 'Are you all packed?' I asked Bull.

'What's to pack?' he said. 'I travel light.'

'We'll leave the guns on our bunks,' I said. 'Maybe the miserable guy who runs the gunshop will buy them back off you.'

'I might just keep them,' Red said. 'Kind of souvenir. And you never know when you'll need a Kalashnikov or a sniper rifle.'

'There is such a thing as being overcautious,' I said.

'And that from a man who buried his Browning,' Bull said.

'Touché,' I said. 'Hang on a minute. I was only following your lead.'

'That's no excuse. I never claimed to be a good role model.' He laughed. 'Still, it's fun being sneaky sometimes.'

'Are you only just discovering that?' Red said.

'I don't have Johnny's experience,' Bull replied.

'Time to go,' I said. 'Before someone else criticizes me.'

I stood up. Shook Stan's and Pieter's hands. Gave them a man-hug. Went off to the bunkhouse to collect my things. Took one last look at the weapons. Hoped I'd never have to pick one up again. That my adventures were over for good, rather than just for the time being.

26

Anna greeted me by jumping into my arms, wrapping her legs around me and giving me the biggest hug and kiss I'd ever had. Coming back makes up for going away.

Life on St Jude slipped into its casual routine. Bull and I would swim along the beach and run back each morning; he would take hotel guests out fishing on his boat; Anna and I would open up our bar/café and give the guests more of the flavour of the Caribbean at half the price. It was idyllic, even more so because I had Anna: life had never been so good.

We set a date and planned the wedding. We would keep it simple and have Bull and his family, the other three guys in the mercenary gang as our guests, together with my mother, Uncle Gus, Scout, Carlo and Natasha. They would all have to stay at the hotel, so we booked that first and worked around available dates. The wedding breakfast would be kept simple, too: a barbecue on the beach with lots of fresh fish, although if Stan got involved there was a likelihood that it would get more complicated, but conducted with military precision — plus pickled gherkins, of course.

By the time of the wedding Anna would be six months pregnant, but she was insistent on wearing a white dress. She went to Barbados with Mai Ling and came back with lots of bags which she hid secretly where I wasn't supposed to find them. In a cabin as small as ours, that was difficult. We would need to start work on a bigger place that would accommodate three of us.

Bull was taking four men from the hotel on a marlin-fishing expedition and I was helping him with the preparations. I carried out a cool bag with beers and soft drinks and added a bottle of Cockspur rum. Anna was putting the finishing touches to some flying-fish sandwiches for their lunch. Bull and I stood on the jetty and looked out at the deep blue sea.

'Do you ever get to wonder,' he said, 'why we ever leave this place?'

'That's two *evers* in the same sentence.'

'Deserves it,' he said.

'You're right,' I said. 'Has to be a really good reason. Apart from one of us, like Red, getting into trouble he can't handle, there isn't anything that would drag me away.'

'Life's good,' he said simply.

'You heard of hubris and nemesis?'

'Who are they? Some new comedy double-act?'

'Hubris means not tempting fate or the

gods. Nemesis is what you get when you do so. The gods pull you back down to earth.'

'What am I supposed to do? Touch wood when I say something good? Cross my fingers?'

'Always best to keep your feet on the ground.'

'If you say so,' he said. 'But it's impossible to do it right here and now when nothing could be better.'

'I know how you feel. Hard for me to see that it can't get even better. A child is going to make a big difference to our lives. Like some sort of fulfilment. I know Anna feels that way and it's hard to disagree. I only hope that I can handle the responsibility. Be a good father.'

'Hell,' he said, 'you'll make a great dad. You're always thinking of other people. That won't change.'

'Pretty scary, though,' I said.

He nodded. 'But good at the same time. Believe me.'

Anna called across to me to tell me she'd finished making the sandwiches. I walked back to the bar and took another cool bag with them inside across to Bull. His guests were walking along the beach. Bull hailed them and started to make preparations for leaving. The men climbed on board and I stood on the jetty, casting off the ropes. I waved them goodbye. Walked back to the bar and stood there talking to Anna. A boat came into view and it moved towards the jetty. A man stepped off, made fast and walked towards the bar. He had on a flowery-print shirt over shorts that came halfway between his shins and his feet. He was wearing small steel-rimmed sunglasses that made him look like a myopic banker in disguise. He came up to the counter and ordered a cold beer. Then I felt the gun in the small of my back.

'Don't try anything funny,' he said, 'or the girl gets it.'

'Hardly an original line,' I said.

'But effective,' he said.

I nodded. No sense denying it. 'The man in black?' I said.

It was his turn to nod. 'Let's move into the shade.'

He turned me round, the gun not wavering from my back and indicated a table at the fringes of the bar. He picked up his beer in his left hand and we moved across to the table. 'Sit over there,' he said. 'Put your hands on the table where I can see them.'

'I'm only wearing a pair of shorts. There's no place to conceal a weapon.'

'Just do as I say,' he said. He levelled the gun at my chest and sat down opposite me, [illegible]t enough out of range of me so that my [illegible]s were nil.

'What brings you here?' I asked.

'I've got a reputation to uphold. Won't do it any good if you beat me and get away with it. Nothing personal, but I'm going to have to kill you.'

'If you're going to kill me, I'd like three last requests.'

'No harm in asking,' he said.

'First, I want your word that the girl is left out of this.'

'It's business,' he said. 'This is only between you and me. What's next?'

'I'd like to see your eyes.'

He smiled and took off his sunglasses. There was that cold glint of steel that I had expected to see.

'Last,' I said, 'I'd like a cold beer. Might as well enjoy my final moments.'

'Not unreasonable,' he said.

I called across to Anna who, having worked out what was going on, was standing shaking at the bar. 'I'd like a cold beer,' I said. 'One of the really cold ones at the base of the refrigerator. When you've got it, you stay behind the bar as safe as you can get. Throw the beer to me. Make it high so that I can catch it easily. Understand?'

'Yes, Johnny,' she said, her voice wavering with fear. 'I understand.'

'Why couldn't you guys have left me

alone?' he said. 'I gave you plenty of warning.'

'As we did you.'

'Cheap tricks; like shooting that tree and attacking the bikers at night. Molotov cocktails.' He shook his head. 'You are one lucky bastard.'

'Looks like my luck has just run out.'

'Reckon so,' he said, stealing my catchphrase.

'I've got your beer, Johnny,' Anna called.

'Do as I said, throw it high.'

'Yes, Johnny.'

She dipped her hand under the bar and sent out a long looping throw. The man in black looked up and was momentarily blinded by the sun. It was all the edge I needed. I caught the Browning in my right hand and in one move aimed it at the man in black's head and shot him between the eyes. He fell backwards and toppled off the chair. I ran across to Anna, opened the counter and put my arms around her. She buried her face in my neck and sobbed, shivering all the time as if she couldn't get rid of the fear.

'You did well,' I said. 'It's all over now. Nothing's going to hurt us.'

She stood up straight and looked me in the eye. 'You were right,' she said.

'Not about the man in black,' I said. 'I thought we'd never see him again. That he had nothing to gain by seeking revenge.'

'Not about that,' she said. 'About the gun. Thank God you didn't throw it into the sea.'

'I wasn't sure you'd get my meaning. I owe my life to you and your quick thinking. Good throw, too.'

'You have my permission to tape it under the bar like you used to.' She gave me a thin smile. 'Hold me tight,' she said. 'I never want to lose you. You're too precious to me.'

I put my arms around her and pressed her body into mine. We must have stayed that way for a full five minutes, unmoving apart from our breathing.

'What are you going to do about that?' she asked, pointing at the man in black's body lying on the sand.

'I'll phone the police on Barbados.' There were no police on St Jude. There was no crime on St Jude. Not until today, that is.

'Pour us both a large measure of rum,' I said. 'Purely medicinal. And before you say anything, one drink won't harm the baby.'

I reached across the bar and picked up my mobile phone. The Barbados police said they'd come straight away. I looked at the body and the thin line of blood staining the sand red. I couldn't very well leave it there like that. Not good for business. I dragged it into the shade behind the bar and covered it with a blanket from our cabin. And that was the end of the man in black.

* * *

The police came by helicopter, took a statement from me and loaded the body on board. Bull arrived back at that precise moment.

He shook his head. 'I can't leave you for a few hours without you leaving dead bodies all over the place.'

'Only the one dead body,' I said.

'I was using the plural for dramatic effect.'

'It worked,' I said.

'How's Anna?'

'She'll be OK. She's a strong woman with a cool head.'

'We were wrong, weren't we?' he said. 'He damn well came back. Is this that hubris thing you talked about?'

'Reckon so,' I said. 'Never anger the gods by showing arrogance or committing the sin of pride.'

'I'll remember that,' he said.

'Pretty hard to forget after today.'

'Reckon so,' he said. 'Is this the end of it?'

'You better believe it. It's the end.'

'Until the next time,' he said.

'Reckon so.'